THE KEEPER

A Short Story

Robert D. Hurley

For my boys,
may you never lose the wonder of it all,
and may you always find the time for a good yarn.

CONTENTS

CHAPTER 1

(Sunday Day 1 / October 11, 2020)

From the shoulder of U.S. Highway 101, just north of Crescent City, Erick sat in his broken-down Mercedes as other motorists raced by. The weather was getting nasty, and if the weatherman's forecast was correct, it would get much worse. A massive storm system had formed to the northwest over the Pacific. All forecast models showed it tracking southeasterly towards northern California. Erick had left Oregon early Monday morning after getting word of his father's death. He was heading home to Rancho Palos Verdes to take care of his father's affairs when his Mercedes decided to make other plans.

Having just called for a tow, he tossed his cell phone onto the dashboard. He watched as raindrops raced sideways across the windshield. Up ahead, he could make out a billboard depicting two lighthouses. It was an advertisement for the Battery Point Lighthouse and the St. George Reef Lighthouse. According to the billboard, both lighthouses were close by and listed as historical landmarks.

Erick had always had an affinity for lighthouses and the stories surrounding them. The fact that his father had shared that same passion only made them more intriguing. Erick supposed a shrink would have thought differently. They probably would have said his attraction to lighthouses had more to do with his mother's death and his father's subsequent absence. That on a subconscious level, his psyche was trying to fill a void. For most, lighthouses symbolized stability and reliability. They were shining lights that never wavered, not even in the worst of life's storms. However, the truth of the matter was that Erick had always admired lighthouses even before his family's disintegration.

After he had gotten word of his father's death, his game plan had been to leave at once in hopes of outrunning the approaching storm, but so go the best laid plans of mice and men. The cars' heater wrapped him in a cozy cocoon of warmth as he listened to the monotonous sound of the rain hitting the roof. Bleary-eyed and yawning, Erick stared at the lighthouse billboard. Exhausted and in need of rest, it was only a matter of time before he succumbed to fatigue and eventually dozed off...

Erick was alone in a wooden rowboat in the middle of a storming sea. It was dark, but there was enough ambient light that he could see the swells were enormous; from trough to crest, he estimated they were between thirty and forty feet. As if his predicament wasn't dire enough, he had been unable to find any oars or life vests on board. He was entirely at the mercy of the sea. Just before the rowboat drifted over another crest, there was light off in the distance. As the little boat climbed the face of the next swell, Erick positioned himself to get another look. As the rowboat floated over the peak and began its descent into the trough, he saw the light again. This time there was no doubt in his mind; it was the beam from a lighthouse. Erick crawled towards the boat's bow and searched the darkness for anything he might use as a makeshift paddle. Finding nothing, he tried hanging his arm over the right side of the boat while clawing at the water with a cupped hand, but it was pointless. Even with oars, his efforts would've proved ineffective in such conditions; he was doing good to keep the boat right side up. Each time the rowboat made it to the next crest, Erick searched the darkness for the distant light before white-knuckling the boat's gunwales for the screaming descent down the other side. As lightning flashed, he heard the thunder roll and crash.

Erick was startled awake by rapping at his driver's side window. Shaking the dreams from his head, he saw a man in a bright yellow rain slicker bent over, tapping his knuckles on the glass, and drawing circles in the air trying to get him to roll down his window. Erick cracked the window, and the man said, "Hey there, my name's Jimmy. You the dude that called for the flatbed?" After confirming he was the one that had called, Jimmy instructed him to sit in the cab of the tow truck while he loaded the car onto the flatbed. "It's company policy, and it's safer for you. Besides, no sense in both of us getting wet," Jimmy had said.

Erick watched from the cab as other drivers raced by with total disregard for the weather and road conditions. As Jimmy secured the vehicle to the flatbed, Erick noticed a pair of approaching headlights drifting out of their lane and towards the shoulder where Jimmy was working. Time seemed to move in slow motion as the errant driver, realizing their mistake, overcompensated and yanked their steering wheel hard to the left. The sudden correction caused the automobile to begin hydroplaning across the wet highway. Meanwhile, having finished strapping the rear wheels, Jimmy began making his way back to the cab. As he rounded the rear quarter panel, he caught a glimpse of the approaching car in his peripheral. Simultaneously, the hydroplaning car careened by as Jimmy dove beneath the flatbed, only just avoiding becoming another highway patrol statistic. Erick watched as the automobile continued sliding across the shoulder, narrowly missing the flatbed's front fender, where it struck the guardrail and careened back towards the highway and into oncoming traffic. The driver and car eventually came to rest facing northbound in the southbound number two-lane. As Jimmy climbed out from under the rear bumper, Erick exited the cab, and began inspecting the condition of his car. "Wow! That was a close one. It doesn't look like they hit us; I don't see any damage." In what appeared to be a mixture of disgust and dismay,

Jimmy shook his head, "yeh, thanks for asking, man. I think I'm okay as well." Oblivious to the tow driver's irritation, Erick returned to the cab and climbed back in. At the same time, Jimmy went to check on the other motorist.

Jimmy and Erick exited Highway 101 and turned down Northcrest Drive. Jimmy said, "we're almost there. Dick's is just up ahead across from the Tire Center. Look, dude, there's something you need to know. Richard's not big on small talk. Sometimes he can be a bit of a hard ass, but he's cool. Whatever you do, don't smudge his windows. For some reason, the man has a thing about his windows. It must be some weird obsessive-compulsive thing. Just don't touch the glass, dude." Erick looked puzzled, "windows? What's that all about?" "I'm not sure, man, but for some reason, the dude has a thing about clean windows. I can't make heads or tails of it myself. Who knows, maybe he was a window cleaner in another life, can't say, it's above my paygrade anyway." Erick nodded his head as if he understood. Jimmy pulled the flatbed into the parking lot and told Erick to go inside while he took his car around back to the work bays.

The shop was a gray-colored building made of metal siding. It had large windowpanes on either side of a glass door. Hanging in the door was a sign that read, "we're open, come on in." Erick had to admit, despite all the rain, these windows were immaculate. The waiting room had several rows of well-worn chairs with end tables littered with magazines at the ends of each row.

Off to the right, in the corner, stood one of those animatronic fortune-telling machines. This machine was different. Erick had seen the old Zoltar machines before, where, for a fee, the turban-wearing fortuneteller would spit out a card with your fortune. This one was called Old Pirate and had a one-eyed animatronic pirate replete with a hook on the one hand and a squawking parrot on his shoulder. Hanging on the opposite wall was a flatscreen television tuned to horse racing. Making his way to the front counter, Erick saw it was a live broadcast from the Santa Anita Park in Arcadia, California. Once he got to the counter, he saw a large man seated at a wooden desk speaking to someone on an old rotary telephone. It had been ages since Erick had seen a rotary phone; those things are dinosaurs, he thought. The large man held up his index finger to let Erick know he would be right with him. As Erick waited, he could hear the race caller at Santa Anita Park announce, "ladies and gentlemen, it is official. The final results of race nine are Seaworthy, Hang-On, and A-Star."

Erick turned back to the counter as the large man hung up the telephone and stood. He was a big guy; Erick would've guessed six foot three inches and close to two hundred and forty pounds. As the two men shook hands, the large man introduced himself as Richard, the owner and chief mechanic. Jimmy, the young man that had towed Erick in, was his apprentice mechanic and handled all the tow truck duties. Richard explained that, based on the information Erick had given over the telephone, it sounded to him that the issue was with the car's driveshaft. He explained that it made sense given there had been a manufacturer recall issued last November. The parts recall had to do with the carbon-fiber driveshaft separating from the engine/transmission flange. Richard explained that he would have to verify his diagnosis by getting the car on the lift so he could take a closer look. "It shouldn't take much more than thirty minutes," he said.

It was evident to Erick that this was not going to be a quick fix. Using his cellphone, he arranged to have a rental vehicle dropped off at the repair shop. With his hands tied, he decided to find a seat and peruse the magazine offerings. He browsed a Sports Illustrated and an old Auto Trader, but neither held his interest. As he sat there dozing off, the fortune-telling machine came to life with a loud shriek from the parrot, "BRAAAACH!" the machine's lights began flashing. The one-eyed pirate came to life, "Take this word from an old pirate and use it fer yer good!" Erick got up and walked over to the animatronic machine and stared at the old pirate incased behind the glass.

Looking down, he saw a cash feed slot with a sign taped above that read, "one dollar per fortune/Absolutely NO refunds." Erick reached in his pocket, peeled off a dollar bill from his money clip, and fed it into the cash slot. The machine grabbed hold of the dollar and came back to life. The pirate winked and looked from left to right nodding his head as he spoke, "Take this word from an old pirate and use it fer yer good.

Heed the fortune I be tellin' and get while the getting's good." All at once, the machine went dark, and the animatronic pirate slumped back into silence. Several seconds later, the machine dispensed a beige card from a slot next to the cash feed slot. Erick pulled the card from the opening and read, "Beware the Keeper's soured rum." The fortune on the card didn't seem to make any sense. Did rum even go sour? Erick heard the door connecting the waiting room and garage open and close.

Erick stuffed the card into his pocket and walked back to the front desk where Richard was waiting. "Well, Mr. Williamson, I have some good news and a little bad news. Which would you like first?" After a moment, Erick said, "please, give me the bad news first; that way, I'll at least have something to look forward to." Richard smiled and said, "well, sir, to begin with, the issue is what we had discussed earlier; it's the carbon-fiber driveshaft separating from the engine flange. The bad news is the part is unique and not something I keep in stock. The good news is I can get the part, and the fix is relatively simple." Richard went on to explain that because it was a manufacturer recall there would be no charge. Erick was more concerned with the time it was going to take to fix his car than about the cost. Richard told him he had spoken with the nearest dealer over in Medford, Oregon, and he had said they could ship it today. Still, because of the storm, they couldn't guarantee a date. Richard estimated it would take anywhere from two to four days. Because business was so slow, he could have the car ready in five to seven hours once he had the part. Richard asked, "so, do I need to call my man in Medford about the part?" Erick cocked his head and sighed, "It doesn't sound like I have any other options, Richard." Richard gave a stern nod with his head, "I'm on it. Grab a seat, and I'll print out a work order."

Turning to find a seat, Erick watched as two cars pulled into the parking lot and parked at the curb in front of the shop. A woman wearing a red sports jacket with a navy-blue skirt exited one of the cars with an umbrella. The red, white, and blue scarf she wore around her neck was flapping in the wind like a flag in a hurricane. The woman opened the umbrella, and the wind unceremoniously turned it inside out. He could read the look of disgust on her face as she threw the umbrella to the ground and stomped away, high heels and all, up onto the concrete walkway under the shop's front overhang. He watched as she took a moment to compose herself before coming inside the shop. Erick rushed over and opened the waiting room door for her.

Stepping inside, she said, "you wouldn't, by any chance, be Mr. Williamson, would you?" Erick smiled and said, "that's me, guilty as charged." Returning his smile, she introduced herself as Joan and explained that she was from the rental agency and was there to drop off his rental car. She produced a file folder holding several papers requiring his signature and initials. After Erick had signed everything, Joan handed him the keys and asked if he would like to inspect the vehicle for damage before she left. Erick grinned and said, "can

I just take your word for it? I don't think either of us wants to be out in this stuff unless we have to be." Joan smiled and nodded, "thank you, Mr. Williamson. It's company policy, so I have to ask, but I was hoping you were going to say that." Joan put the papers back into the folder and said, "goodbye, sir, and thank you for your business." He watched her exit the shop and scamper over to the second car.

As the two agents drove away, Richard called him back to the front counter with more paperwork that required his signature. As Erick signed the work order, Richard leaned over the counter and said, "you know, since you're going to be in town for a few days, you might want to stay someplace a little nicer than a hotel or motel." Erick looked up and thought for a minute, "you know Richard, that's not a bad idea. Do you have something in mind?" Richard grinned, "you bet, Aunt Mabel's B&B over on W. Ninth Street. Aunt Mabel's has, without a doubt, the best accommodations in town. Prices are very reasonable, and the meals are all home-cooked. It's like dinner and a show over there; you'll see what I mean." Richard glanced over at an old Coors Banquet beer wall clock hanging above his desk, "I'm sure one of the sisters is up and about over there. I'll write the directions on the back of your copy of the work order." Erick thanked him but explained all he needed was the address to program into his cellphone's GPS.

Despite the wind and rain, Aunt Mabel's B&B was easy enough to find. Erick followed his GPS directions down Highway 101 to where it forked. Taking the fork on the right, he made a right on the next street, Ninth Street. After negotiating some mild flooding by the middle school, he continued down Ninth Street to what appeared to be some type of memorial called Brother Jonathan Park. Aunt Mabel's B&B was across the street just north of the park. To the west, just across S. Pebble Beach Drive, were bluffs that led down to the Pacific Ocean; the view was spectacular. Erick parked along the curb in front of the two-story Victorian-style house.

A small yet well-manicured lawn surrounded the house with well-trimmed shrubs beneath a bay window adjacent to the front porch. The wood siding was painted white, and the roof was a dark, somewhat grayish slate. The gable above the front porch had small carved decorative ornaments that Erick couldn't quite make out. The two newel posts, flanking the steps leading to the front porch, were fashioned as lighthouses, with the finials acting as the lighthouse lanterns. The steps led to a modest front porch and a front door painted black. Erick exited the rental car and trotted across the sidewalk and up the front steps to the front porch. Standing in front of the front door, he took a moment to shake the rain off his clothing. The upper half of the front door had a large glass insert with sheer white window curtains draped to either side hanging from the inside. A sign next to the front door read, "Let us welcome you home to Aunt Mabel's Bed & Breakfast where everyone's family." Erick rang the doorbell below the sign.

As soon as he rang the doorbell, a small dog began barking from just inside. From behind the door, Erick heard a woman's voice scold the dog, "Bear-Bear, you hush a minute!" A few moments later, a tall woman wearing reading glasses and holding an overly excited brown poodle opened the front door. The lady introduced herself as Shirley Bradley and introduced the lively poodle as Sir Barrymore Jr. She looked to be in her mid to late sixties and spoke with a slight southern drawl. After introducing himself, Erick explained his situation and asked if they had any rooms available. Shirley explained that because it was their off-season, she could pretty much guarantee they had a room for him. Shirley said he would have to speak with her sister first because Mabel took care of that side of the business. Shirley explained that Mabel would be back shortly; she had just run out to take care of a couple of errands. Shirley told Erick to go ahead and grab any luggage he had and put it next to the stairs, and she would go and put some coffee on.

Erick had just finished his first cup of coffee when Mabel pulled up the driveway, parking at the back-porch stairs in front of the garage. Shirley got up from the wingback chair, "excuse me, I had best run and help Mabel bring in the groceries." Erick offered to help, but Shirley wouldn't have it. "Nope, not a chance, especially with you about to be a paying guest. I reckon we can hold off putting you to work 'til we've collected your check," she said with a wink and a sly grin. As Shirley left the room Sir Barrymore Jr. jumped to his feet, and let out a yapp before chasing off after her.

A few minutes later, a woman entered the room and introduced herself as Mabel Bradley, the owner and proprietor of Aunt Mabel's Bed & Breakfast. Mabel explained that her sister Shirley helped with some of the chores and maintenance but that she handled the business end of the arrangement. As they finished the paperwork, Mabel explained that dinner was usually around six o'clock in the evening, "unless I'm dead..." she had joked,"...in which case, there'll be leftovers in the fridge, so help yourself. I hope you have a sweet tooth, Mr. Williamson, because I always serve dessert with dinner." As Mabel led Erick up the stairs to his room, she added, "Also, if you have any food restrictions, best tell me now. I sure don't want to feed you my peanut butter pie if you have a nut allergy." Mabel took Erick to the largest of the four bedrooms in the house.

The bedroom was right next to the bathroom and faced the front of the house. From his bedroom window, he could see the Park across the street. There was a wooden console table in front of the window with two tiffany table lamps, one at each end. On the wall to the left of the window, a familiar painting reproduction caught his eye; it was one of his favorites. The painting was by American impressionist Frank Weston Benson and was titled "Summer." The piece captured four young ladies in long white dresses as they leisurely enjoyed a sunny day from atop a seaside bluff. Though he couldn't explain why, Erick had always imagined the four ladies to be sisters. Examining the room, he also noticed several old black and white tintype photographs hanging on the wall adjacent to the bedroom door. In the corner, next to the bed and nightstand, was a wooden accent chair.

The house had beautiful wood flooring, which was accented using large space rugs for comfort and decor. When Erick asked Mabel about the old photographs, she told him, "they came with the house. Seeing as how they were here long before us; it didn't seem right to take them down. Besides, they add to the character, don't you think?" Erick nodded his head, "they certainly do fit right in with the lighthouse theme." Mabel smiled and told Erick she would leave him to settle in while she went down and got dinner started. On her way out, she smiled and said, "you know Mr. Williamson, we hardly get any boarders in the offseason. It's a stroke of fate that you found us." Erick smiled, "Ms. Bradley, I'm just thankful I was able to find such nice accommodations on such short notice, and please, I would appreciate you and your sister calling me Erick." Returning his smile, Mabel said, "likewise sweetheart; from here on out, it's Mabel, Shirley, and Bear-Bear. See you at dinner." Closing the bedroom door behind her, Mabel left for the kitchen, and Erick began to unpack his clothes to change into something dry. He wanted to see if he could squeeze a nap in before dinner.

Over dinner, Erick shared everything he had been through since getting the news of his father's death. When he had finished, he sat silently staring at the glass of sweet tea sitting in front of him on the table.

Using his index finger Erick wiped the tiny droplets of condensation from the sides of his drinking glass, "don't get me wrong, I loved my father, it's just...I don't know, it's like I never really got to know the man. After mom, everything changed. Have you ever had thoughts you mistook for memories only to find out later that you imagined them?" Shirley wiped the corners of her mouth and returned her table napkin to her lap, "Erick, I truly am sorry for your loss. It's best not to overthink such matters. You've had a long day and have been through the wringer. No doubt, you are worn-out. It's probably best to sleep on it and look with fresh eyes in the morning."

Shirley added, "Mabel told me you were admiring the photographs in your room earlier." Erick replied, "yes, yes, I was. They're fascinating and look like they're antiques." Shirley went on to expound on Mabel's earlier comments that the photographs and the house, for that matter, were from the 1800s. She explained how most lighthouse keepers had been allowed to have their families living with them while they served, but not those posted on St. George Reef. Because of the hazardous conditions out on the Reef, a keepers' family had to live on the mainland. This old Victorian house that is now Aunt Mabel's B&B had, at one time, been a keeper's home. "So, you see, the old tintype photos are as much a part of the house as the wood floors. In fact, there are a couple of old pieces of furniture from that time as well; that oak dresser in your room is one such piece."

While Shirley talked, Mabel refilled Erick's plate

with Chicken-Fried Steak, Redeye Gravy, green beans, and two homemade biscuits. Mabel positioned the plate in front of Erick with a sympathetic smile, "you sit right there and finish your dinner. When you're finished, there's a banana pudding in the fridge. You can help yourself." Erick smiled and thanked Mabel as he pushed away from the table. Patting his protruding belly, he politely begged off the second helping. But only after Mabel had made him promise to try her banana pudding the following day. Exhausted, Erick said goodnight before excusing himself and retreating to his bedroom.

CHAPTER 2

The following morning Erick woke to the smell of bacon and fresh homemade buttermilk biscuits. After a quick shower and shave, he followed his nose to the kitchen where breakfast was already underway, "good morning Mr. Williamson," Shirley said. "Please, Shirley, call me Erick, remember?" Shirley nodded her head, "right you are, my mistake. Did you sleep well?" Erick sat down and placed both hands on the kitchen table before registering an emphatic, "yes, between the rain and my exhaustion, I slept like a champ. I feel great this morning." Both sisters smiled in approval. Mabel took a cast iron skillet from the stovetop and placed it on a trivet at the table's center. Shirley leaned over the table as if she had a secret to divulge, "I'm not sure if you're aware of this Erick, but Mabel's buttermilk biscuits are the pride of Etowah County; that's in Alabama, of course. Nobody, and I stress nobody, makes a better biscuit than Mabel." Mabel turned back towards the stove, visibly embarrassed by such high praise, shaking her head, "Lord have mercy, Shirley Dean, you must be blind in one eye and not able to see out the other!" Shirley looked at Erick with raised eyebrows and shrugged her shoulders as if she were surprised by Mabel's reaction to her extravagant praise. Erick just grinned; he found their bantering back and forth humorous. Now he understood what Richard had meant about dinner and a show. Truth be told, Erick was a little envious of their close relationship. Sometimes he had wondered what it would've been like to have a sibling. With everything that was going on in his life, it would've been nice to have someone to commiserate with.

Shirley pinched a piece from a strip of bacon and tossed it under the table where Sir Barrymore Jr. had been quietly waiting, "so what's on your agenda for the day, Erick?" Erick thought for a moment, "well, I guess I better touch base with Richard and get an update on my car. Everything hinges on the shipping of that part." Shirley tossed another piece of bacon under the table, "the reason I ask is it looks like the rain has let up. Might be a good opportunity for some sightseeing."

Erick recalled the billboard on the highway from the day before, "now that you mention it, I did see a billboard advertisement for two lighthouses here in Crescent City. I am admittedly a bit of a lighthouse enthusiast." Shirley nodded her head and said, "yes, sir, you would be referring to the Battery Point Lighthouse down at the harbor and the St. George Reef Lighthouse out at The Dragon Rocks. The Battery Point Lighthouse is still a working lighthouse, so you might be able to get a tour. Unfortunately, the St. George Reef Lighthouse is about six miles west of Point St. George in the Pacific Ocean. Not real hospitable waters this time of year, especially with that storm sitting out there. If you're really interested, you should head over to Battery Point. I'm sure one of the keeps over there will be able to fill you in."

Erick went into the living room and plopped down on one of the tall wingback chairs that sat at either side of the large bay window to the house's front. Looking out the window, Erick could see that Shirley had been right; the rain had indeed subsided, and the sun was out. It looked like it was going to be a beautiful day. Grabbing his cell phone, he punched in the numbers for Dick's Auto Repair and was caught slightly off guard when Richard answered before the first ring, "I was just about to call you. I checked with the dealership in Medford, Oregon, this morning. Under normal circumstances, they could have the part here in five or six hours, but with this storm wreaking havoc up and down the coast, there's no telling how long it will take. I'll be sure to keep you in the loop, though." While he was on his cellphone, the sisters had entered the living room with their coffee. Erick ended his call and closed his phone with a sigh, "well ladies, it doesn't look like I'm going anywhere today. That is if you'll have me, of course." With feigned irritation, Shirley rolled her eyes and let out an exaggerated sigh of annoyance, "there goes my Monday." Looking up from the scrabble board on the coffee table, Mabel responded, "Shirley Dean, you hush now. Erick, honey, never mind Shirley, she's just being ornery. You can stay as long as you want sweetheart, we enjoy having you." Erick smiled and thanked the sisters for their gracious hospitality. He couldn't recall ever feeling so welcomed in someone's home and even had to resist the urge to give them a hug. Erick had no doubt that Mabel and Shirley were the genuine articles. The sisters were indeed the embodiment of what he had always imagined a doting grandmother would be like. Stranded for at least two more days, Erick decided to check out the Battery Point lighthouse Shirley had been telling him about at breakfast. Excusing himself, he left the sisters to their game of Scrabble while he headed out to do a little sightseeing.

Following his cellphone's GPS, Erick drove to the end of Lighthouse Way and parked in a small public parking lot. Standing next to his car, he could see the B Street Jetty stretching out towards the mouth of the harbor. Further to the jetty's right was the breakwater and then an island with several structures, one being a lighthouse. Erick assumed this was the Battery Point lighthouse he kept hearing about. The lighthouse was of the Cape Cod-style, where the tower and lantern extend up and out of the roof of the keeper's living quarters. This style of lighthouse Erick recognized. He had seen it in some of the old 1890's photos his father had collected.

He had seen this style again when his family had visited the Old Point Loma Lighthouse in San Diego.

As he stood there, a tall, burly man walked up and asked, "can I help you there?" The man wore a navy-blue watch cap over a thickly woven matching wool sweater. His wiry hair and beard were dark with glints of gray here and there. Everything about the man, style, demeanor, and even the burlap bag he had slung over his shoulder suggested a seafaring occupation. Erick told the man, "I had hoped to tour the lighthouse." Scratching the side of his beard, the man replied, "that's not gonna happen today. Tours are permitted by tidal invitation only." Erick wasn't sure, but he thought he had detected, if only for a second, the ghost of a grin pass across the man's lips, but it was difficult to say because of the bushy beard. Nodding towards the lighthouse, and perhaps sensing Erick's confusion, the man clarified, "You can only access the island at low tide when the walkway is accessible." Erick raised his head to indicate he understood, "that's too bad; I wish I had more time; I had hoped to see it." The man smiled and extended his hand, "the name's John, John Eldin. I'm the Keeper at Battery Point. If it were left to me, I'd ferry you across in my skiff. Unfortunately, it's against the regs, and with the heightened state of alert everybody has their drawers all knotted up on account of the storm, it would be a bad idea." As soon as Erick took hold of the man's calloused hand, he could feel the power in the grip. Unlike Erick, this man was accustomed to back-breaking labors. Erick introduced himself and told the man he didn't want to get him into trouble. The man glanced at the lighthouse and then back at Erick before saying, "you know, just because I can't give you the full tour doesn't mean I can't give you the abridged version." Erick smiled and said, "I'm all ears."

John rummaged through his gunny sack and pulled out an old dented green thermos with a silver lid. He poured the steaming liquid into the silver cup and offered it to Erick. Erick declined, and John raised the cup and nodded his head, "cheers." After replacing the stopper in the thermos, he stuffed it back in the sack. John turned around towards the Battery Point lighthouse and took a sip of coffee before beginning.

John Eldin explained how the Battery Point Lighthouse had gotten its unusual name. A battery of cannons had been mounted on the harbor's northeast side. Every year they would fire the three Large guns as part of the traditional Fourth of July celebration. The cannons had been salvaged from America's shipwreck, which had burned in the harbor in 1855. As for the lighthouse, the original lamp had been a Fourth-Order Fresnel lens. The light was first lit on December 10, 1856. Ninety-seven years later, in 1953, the light was automated and eventually deactivated in 1965. John stretched out his arm and pointed southeast of the lighthouse, "Her replacement is out there on the breakwater, but we don't speak of her." Turning his attention back to the Battery Point lighthouse, John continued, "The living quarters are comfortable enough. The walls are granite stone, whereas the tower is brick. She was relit in 1982, but only as a personal directional aid." Turning back towards Erick, John said, "that's about all there is to tell unless you're wanting to hear ghost stories. While I don't go in for such things myself, I have heard others make claims. I suppose it adds to the mystique. I'm sure you know all about the harbor waves or tsunamis. We've had a few, but the one in 1964 was the worst. As I recall, it killed eleven people and pretty much destroyed the city. If you get a chance, head over to the Del Norte County Historical Society Museum in town. They have loads of historical information on the area, and especially on the two lighthouses." Erick thanked John and watched as the man slung his gunny sack over his shoulder and trudged down the narrow path that led between the jagged rocks of the cliff. Before he was out of view, John shouted back, "Fair winds and following seas!"

Using the directions John Eldin had given him, Erick drove up H street and parked near a white building with a wooden sign on the front lawn that read MUSEUM in bold white lettering. Exiting his car, he walked to the front door. A second sign identified the building as the *Del Norte County Historical Museum* just above the front door. Erick took ahold of the doorknob and gave it a turn, but nothing happened. He jiggled it back and forth, and still nothing. That's when he noticed a sign sitting on the window ledge, just inside, announcing, "Closed for renovations." A bit disheartened by his lack of luck, Erick peered in through a window.

From his vantage point, he could see what looked to be Native American baskets, needlework, and musical instruments. Erick also noticed some old military and mining artifacts. As he scanned the room's contents, his eyes were drawn to a second window on the far side of the room. Through the other window, Erick could see a second white-colored building behind the museum. Pushing away from the window, he walked around the building to where he had seen the second building. Walking up to the front door, Erick grabbed the doorknob and gave it a turn. To his surprise, the knob turned.

As the front door swung, open Erick felt a gust of cold, stale air. Walking through the doorway and into the building, he saw a man standing in the center of the room facing the opposite direction, "hello...excuse me...the door was —" "Unlocked? Yes, lad, of that I'm well aware, for I made it so. Come in, come in!"

As the man slowly turned, Erick was impressed by the immaculate state of his uniform. The ten golden buttons adorning his double-breasted navy-blue coat had been polished to a luster. Each button reflected the sunlight shining through the window over Erick's shoulder. The man wore a navy-blue bell-cap with two golden branches curved in an upward arc embroidered at the center of the cap's face. Between the golden branches stood a silver embroidered lighthouse emblem. The gold and silver contrasting with the navy-blue of the bell-cap were exquisite. As the man smiled and stretched out his arm to shake hands, Erick could see two more golden buttons on the sleeve, with four gold, embroidered hash marks, each about an inch apart. Embroidered just above the top hash on either sleeve sat a final silver lighthouse for good measure.

Shaking the man's hand, Erick immediately thought of John Eldin back at Battery Point, as both men had heavily calloused and extremely firm grips. "Welcome to the Bolen Annex, lad. Pleased to make yer acquaintance. Jack Duffy's the name, I'm the annex curator." Erick replied, "pleased to meet you, Mr. Duffy. My name is Erick Williamson." Curator Duffy slowly nodded his head up and down, as if the two men shared a secret, before saying, "well, of course, you are. Glad to have you back aboard, lad." Before Erick could ask what he meant by "back aboard," the curator had spun around with his arm extended and said, "feel free to look around, plenty to catch yer eye 'round here. I dare say, you picked a perfect day for it, nary a soul in sight."

The curator ascended the staircase and disappeared around the building's largest exhibit, an enormous First-Order Fresnel lens. Erick walked around the impressive light marveling at the workmanship that went into constructing such a device. The light itself was larger than a grown man. The information placards identified the lens as the original lens that lit the St. George Reef Lighthouse from October 20, 1892, until it was decommissioned in 1975. In 1983 the 6,000-pound lamp was moved to the Bolen Annex, where it was placed on display.

Making his way around the exhibits, Erick noticed

three young boys off by themselves sitting on a bench next to a large wooden ship's wheel. Studying the boys, he sensed something was off. For one thing, there wasn't any of the typical horseplay one might expect from three young boys; these kids weren't even fidgeting. No, Erick thought, something was wrong here; this wasn't normal behavior. He noted they bore an uncanny resemblance to one another and therefore assumed they were most likely brothers. Like statues in their own exhibit, the three boys sat on their bench staring at Erick but giving no indication that they were seeing him; it was as if they were looking through him.

Erick shrugged it off and dismissed his critique as unwarranted, and scolded himself for thinking something was off about three young boys behaving themselves in public. Still, he couldn't deny that feeling...the intuition that shouted there was something peculiar about these boys.

Erick could see an old tintype photograph hanging on the wall behind the ship's wheel. The picture depicted a group of ten men dressed in their Sunday best and wearing black bowler hats. Examining the wheel in the photograph, he saw it bore the same inscription as the wheel on display in the exhibit. Both had the same words across their felloes, "Brother Jonathan wrecked July 30th, 1865." *The two wheels are one and the same*, he thought. As Erick stood staring at the old photograph, he had the uneasy feeling that the ten men gathered around the wheel were staring back at him. A chill ran up the back of his spine, causing him to lift his shoulders and shudder at the thought. Alomost instantly all the windowpanes in the annex began rattling as a crash of thunder reverberated from outside. Startled by the thunder, Erick suppressed a scream as his entire body momentarily tensed up. Recognizing it was about to start raining again, he decided it was time to head back to the car. As he made his way to the door, he was surprised to find he was the only person left in the museum. The three boys had left their bench, and curator Duffy was nowhere to be found. Erick exited the annex through the same door he had entered as an icy gust of wind greeted him as he stepped outside. "A little reminder of the monster yet to arrive," he thought. Dashing for the car, he dug through his pockets keys just as it began to rain again.

In the three-minutes it took Erick to drive the mile between the Bolen Annex and Aunt Mabel's B&B, the rain had turned to a torrential downpour. It was raining so hard Erick could hardly gauge where the curb was to park in front of the house. Without an umbrella, not that it would've mattered since the wind was blowing the rain sideways, he was going to have to sprint for the front porch. He exited the car in one fluid movement and pivoted towards the trunk while slinging his door shut with his trailing hand. Rounding the bumper, he saw the gutter had flooded into the street. Thinking quick, he made the decision to jump the distance to the sidewalk. Using the car's trunk for leverage, he leaped into the air and cleared the obstacle with relative ease. Unfortunately, his landing wasn't as graceful.

Both feet flew out from beneath him as he landed on the slick soles of his fancy leather shoes. He fell back onto his back with a thud that shook the fillings in his molars. With no air left in his lungs, Erick rolled back and forth on the sidewalk holding himself. The only audible words he could muster were high-pitched whimpers. He sounded more like a constipated *Oompa-Loompa* in some deranged remake of *Willy Wonka and the Chocolate Factory*. Mabel and Shirley had witnessed everything from the bay window. Both sisters had been watching, one in horror the other in somber amusement, as Erick's ill-advised leap had ended in abject disaster. As he laid there staring at the clouds, Shirley's face appeared on the left, and then Mabel's appeared on the right. Staring down at him, Shirley finally said, "well, Erick, I have to say you might have scored higher had you stuck the landing. As it is, I give you a solid seven for the effort." The sisters each grabbed an arm and helped him to his feet as Mabel said, "Shirley Dean, behave. Erick, sweetheart, are you okay? Say something." Still struggling for air, Erick just closed his eyes and let the sisters guide him into the house and the living room sofa.

Shirley and Erick sat in the living room while Mabel went to make some coffee. "Mabel fetch a towel while you're out there," Shirley said as she hoisted Sir Barrymore Jr. onto her lap. Shirley looked at Erick and shook her head back and forth slowly, "Lord have mercy, haven't seen anyone hit that hard since Bama's linebacker clobbered that Penn State kid on the goal line back in the '79 Sugar Bowl." Shirley leaned forward and scrunched her nose, "That must've hurt...did it?" Her sorrowful eyes were in contrast with her matter of fact delivery. It was difficult for Erick to tell if she was simply stating the obvious or having a little fun at his expense. From what he knew of Shirley, Erick concluded it was probably a bit of both, with the majority being the former, of course. Having caught his breath, Erick replied, "that definitely did not go as I had planned it. To answer your question, yes, it most certainly did hurt." Shirley leaned back and continued stroking Sir Barrymore Jr. and nodding her head in affirmation, "I figured as much." After a thoughtful pause and with great satisfaction, Shirley added, "yes, sir, Bama won that one 14-7, giving the Bear his fifth national championship."

Mabel entered the room holding a tray of cups, a pot of coffee, and a folded towel over her shoulder. Setting the tray on the coffee table, she turned and handed Erick the towel from her shoulder, "here you go, honey, dry your hair and get you some coffee. I've got some soup on the stove that's almost done; are you hungry?" Erick took the towel and thanked Mabel for the towel and coffee. As he began drying his hair, he told Mabel, "soup sounds great after today, but I'll wait until it's done. Besides, I have a few things I want to run by you ladies." As Erick dried himself and collected his thoughts, he listened as Shirley and Mabel bantered back and forth about stories from their youth. "Mabel, do you remember the story about mama and the milking cow? The one where she nailed the cow's tail to the barn on account of how the cow kept lashing its tail and hitting mama on the head while she milked her?" Mabel leaned back and giggled like a schoolgirl, "Oh my goodness, and how she forgot about it after the milking; and darned if that old cow didn't walk off leaving her tail hanging on the barn for granddaddy to find." Shirley slowly shook her head with a woeful look, "luckily mama was tough as a pine knot 'cause grandaddy skinned her hide and nailed it to the barn door. Yes sir, that story and the whoopin' that followed are legendary amongst kinfolk back in Boaz."

Erick laid the towel across his knee and poured some coffee into one of the cups on the tray. After a few sips, he leaned back and began sharing the events of his day. First, he mentioned his conversation with John Eldin in the parking lot near the Battery Point lighthouse. He explained why he had been unable to take the tour but how Keeper Eldin had happened along and been kind enough to accommodate him with the abridged version. However, when he started telling them about the Bolen Annex and curator Duffy, there was a noticeable change in the sisters. Shirley froze mid-drink and returned her coffee cup to the tray. At the same time, Mabel nervously brushed sofa cushions trying to smooth out wrinkles that were never there. Cocking her head to the side, Shirley cut her eyes over the frame of the bifocals perched on the bridge of her nose, "no offense Erick, but that's not possible." Erick smiled and held up his palms, "none taken Shirley, but I did shake the man's hand, and I did view the exhibits; well, at least those in the annex, the main museum was closed." "Erick," Shirley said, "that's not possible because the museum and the annex have both been closed for renovations since last year's fire." Now it was Erick who was confused. In a soft voice, Mabel awkwardly said, "it's true, honey, both museums are closed. That's why we didn't mention them when we told you about the Battery Point Lighthouse. We knew they would be closed," Erick ran an unsteady hand through his damp hair, "but...I wasn't alone; there were three young boys...on the bench...over by the wheel." When Erick mentioned the three boys, Shirley sat up straight and placed Sir Barrymore Jr. on the floor. Dejected, the little dog wandered off to the kitchen with his muzzle dragging. Shirley said, "Erick, I'm friends with the folks that work at the museum, and Jack Duffy is not a name I'm familiar with. As a matter of fact, there is no 'curator' as such, just the Historical Society. To the best of my recollection, not one of the folks that work the museum has ever worn a uniform. You know, that uniform you just described sounds an awful lot like the ones regulated for the U.S. Lighthouse Service back in the 1800s." In silence, Erick stared at the coffee table and the tray of cups. His mind scrambled to understand as he balanced what the sisters were telling him with all he had experienced earlier in the day. Erick thought, was there some way I imagined it all? Shirley asked, "you sure you didn't bump your noggin in that tumble you just took? It was a pretty hard one?" With his gaze never leaving the tray of cups, Erick began feeling the back of his head. He hoped for a lump, really he did, because the only other explanation would be that he was losing his mind. But Erick knew before his hand ever went up to his head, there would be no lump; after all, that would've been too easy.

There was no rational explanation for what Erick had experienced in light of what Shirley and Mabel had just shared. Mabel excused herself to check on their soup, leaving Erick and Shirley to ponder in silence. Erick broke the silence first, "I trust you're telling me the truth, and I know I'm not lying. I'm sure there's a rational explanation that accounts for everything." Shirley leaned to one side with her elbow on top of the wingback chair's arm. Looking out of the corner of her eyes, she said, "I have a theory. One I dare say could explain all of this, but I don't know that you've a mind to hear it." Erick's impatience got the better of him, "Shirley, you are a very nice woman, and I like you a lot, but if you've got something to say, please just say it." Still looking at him from the corner of her eyes, Shirley asked, "do you believe in a spirit world, Erick?" Erick paused for a minute to think about what Shirley was actually asking. With a half-grin, Erick replied, "I guess that all depends. What exactly do you mean when you say, 'spirit world?' Are you asking whether or not I believe in ghosts?" With the dead-eyed stare of a seasoned poker player, Shirley said, "yes, sir, that's exactly what I'm asking." Seeing the seriousness in Shirley's demeanor, Erick's grin slowly changed from one of amusement to one of nervous unease. Shirley continued, "there's a lot you've yet to hear and read, but we can delve into all that after dinner. Best you go get cleaned up for supper before Mabel calls." Erick agreed and excused himself heading upstairs for the bathroom.

After dining on the most incredible vegetable soup, Mabel chased Erick and Shirley out of the kitchen. She insisted they take their desserts, banana pudding from the night before, and coffees out to the living room and leave her to finish up with the dishes. Erick chose one of the two wingbacks next to the bay window. As he sat down, he noticed a manila envelope sitting on the coffee table. Erick leaned forward and placed his cup of coffee on a coaster next to the envelope. Nodding towards the envelope, he asked, "Is this related to what we were talking about before dinner?" Shirley nodded yes, "there are things inside there you need to see. But they can wait 'til I clean this bowl." Erick had to admit, Mabel's menu was first-rate southern fare.

After their desserts, Shirley opened the manila envelope, "you mentioned you saw 'a wheel,' I think I heard you say?" Erick nodded, "that's right. There was an exhibit with a large ship's wheel." Shirley next asked, "can you recall anything about the ship's wheel." Erick gave it some thought before saying, "Actually yes, the wheel had an inscription across the face of the felloe. It was the name 'Brother Jonathan' with a date from the 1860s." Shirley nodded, explaining he had described the wheel recovered from the Brother Jonathan's shipwreck back on July 30, 1865. Retrieving a piece of paper from the manila envelope, Shirley begins reading,

"The Brother Jonathan, a dual paddle steamer, had left San Francisco Bay on July 28, 1865, at noontime for Portland, Oregon. As soon as the ship left the bay and turned north, she was confronted with intense seas and a fierce headwind. The weather and seas continued to worsen the further north they went. Because of the seas and relentless headwind, the going was slow and arduous. On July 29th at two o'clock in the morning, Captain DeWolf brought the ship into Crescent City Harbor, where he unloaded some of the cargo. By nine-thirty that morning, the ship was back underway. Aware of the 'Dragon Rocks' of St. George's Reef, the captain decided to take a more westerly direction to go around the reef. Avoiding the reef but making little to no progress north because of the heavy seas and unusually powerful headwinds, Captain DeWolf determined it was best to return to the safety of Crescent City Harbor to wait out the storm. At or about noontime, the captain took a sun sight and plotted their position as four miles north of Point St. George. The captain ordered a ship's mate to prepare the bow anchor just in case. While readying the anchor, the mate saw a rock just below the surface and tried to warn the wheelhouse. Unfortunately, his yells weren't in time, as a massive wave lifted the ship and dropped her onto the jagged rock. The relentless waves continued to drive the vessel forward onto the rocky outcrop until she had a gaping hole from her foremast to the bridge."

Shirley looked up from the document and looked

Erick straight in the eye, "only nineteen souls made it off the Brother Jonathan that day. Five women, three children, ten crewmen, and a Third Mate named Mr. Patterson. They were the only ones that made it back to Crescent City Harbor that day to tell the tale of the 225 that perished out on that reef." Shirley went on to tell how the locals had attempted to mount rescue efforts but were forced back by the ferociousness of the seas and wind. She told Erick the Brother Jonathan tragedy was the spark that led to the eventual construction of the St. George Reef Lighthouse on West Seal Rock, "you know Erick, St. George's Reef has a deadly history both before and since the Brother Jonathan tragedy; I dare say it will continue. Make no mistake, that Reef is cursed."

Shirley explained how many believed Sir Francis Drake, or "The Dragon," as the Spanish had called him, had encountered the Reef during his 1579 voyage up the west coast of North America. According to Shirley, many believed it was Drake, and not captain George Vancouver in 1792, that had given the Reef it's menacing nickname "The Dragon Rocks." Leaning forward, Shirley squinted her eyes and began tapping her forefinger to her temple, "it just makes more sense to me. Especially given the nickname the Spanish had given Drake. Still, in the end, I suppose it's six of one and half dozen of the other. Point being it's always been a dangerous place for mariners." With that said, Shirley glanced at the clock on the wall, "Pardon me, Erick, we'll have to continue this later. Mabel and I have to get our *Wheel of Fortune* fix for the day. I always thought *Pat* and *Vanna* made such a cute couple. Mabel has a thing for *Alex Trebek*, so we have to watch *Jeopardy* as well." Erick grinned and said, "sure, we can talk tomorrow. Besides, I'm pretty tired; I think I'm going to call it a night." Erick excused himself and wandered into the kitchen. He thanked Mabel for another excellent meal and complimented her on her banana pudding. Mabel had a smile from ear to ear, "thank you for saying, sweetie. You are most welcome. Don't forget, there are plenty of leftovers; just come on down." Erick told both sisters goodnight and went upstairs to have a long soak in a hot bath before bed.

After his bath, Erick climbed into bed. It had been a long and exciting day. He pulled the blankets up and grimaced as a sharp spike of pain shot across his ribs and lower back. The hot bath had helped, but he was still noticeably sore from his earlier fall. He reached over to the nightstand and turned off the tiffany night-lamp. Erick laid there listening to the rain hitting the roof while the occasional thunderclap rumbled across the sky. He recalled how, as a child, his mother had told him the story of Rip Van Winkle. He recalled how Mr. Winkel discovered thunder due to a group of colorfully clad bearded men playing nine-pins atop a plateau in the mountains. The rolling thunder was caused by errant balls rolling down the plateau and bouncing off rocks, or so the story went. Erick's head was reeling with all he had learned. He still didn't know what to make of Shirley asking him if he believed in ghosts or not. Rehashing all the information was exhausting and more than a little overwhelming. Like a man stuck in quicksand, the more he struggled, the deeper he sank. As fatigue set in, Erick eventually surrendered to sleep and slipped below the surface, and dreamed...

He found himself standing on a wooden ship deck in the middle of a storm. He struggled to keep his balance as the deck heaved up and then down before abruptly rolling to the right causing him to stumble and fall. The heavy seas crashed against the side of the ship's hull, creating a salty mist, and if that weren't enough, there was a thick fog to deal with as well. Looking up, Erick saw a life-ring mounted on a nearby wall above his head. Grabbing hold of the ring, he was able to claw back to his feet. Printed across the life-ring were the words "S.S. Brother Jonathan." Holding to the life-ring for support, He was able to spy through a nearby window and into the large upper deck dining salon. Inside the salon, he saw a hundred or so passengers doing their best to convince and reassure one another that everything was fine. But Erick could read the truth written on their faces; they knew the situation was grave. As he watched the passengers, he could feel the ship heave forward and begin to roll to the starboard, as if going down a slide sideways. By the time he realized what was happening, it was too late. The enormous wave appeared from out of the fog and broadsides the ship smashing him against the wall and knocking him to his knees. Disoriented, Erick felt his body sliding across the deck. He fumbled for anything to hold onto as the retreating water pushed him to the ship's rail. Luckily, a young sailor standing nearby grabbed his pant leg, arresting his slide. With each using the other for support, the two men managed to get back to their feet. Before Erick could thank him, the young sailor was spun around by one of the officers. Holding the young sailor by the lapels, the officer yanked him close until their faces were but inches apart. With a wild look in his eyes and water running down his face, the officer yells, "See here! The Captain has brought us about; we've a new heading! We are to make for the protection of Crescent Harbor until this screaming bitch blows over! The Captain obliges you to make ready with the bow anchor until his order! Do you understand?!" As the deck continues to heave and roll, the two men stand staring at each other, "Aye-aye Mr. Patterson."

Erick followed the young sailor to the foredeck, where he found the roll and heave so intense he was scarcely able to stand. He clutched at the rigging hanging from the foremast and wrapped one of the thick ropes around his arm. He watched as the young sailor readied the ship's anchor by unplugging the hawser hole. As the young man reached through the hole to attach the hawser cable to the eye of the anchor, he suddenly turned back towards the wheelhouse and yelled, "Rocks to port—!" Before he could finish his alert, a huge wave lifted the vessel high and then crashed it down hard onto the rocks the young sailor had tried to warn of. Erick could feel the teeth jarring vibration as it traveled through the foremast. The unmistakable sound of wood crunching and splintering beneath them was horrific. Erick watched as the young sailor collapsed against the port gunwale, his shoulders hunched forward. With a blank stare and ashen face of quiet resignation, the young sailor stared at Erick and said, "well, that'll be it then!" Relentlessly, waves surged the vessel forward, driving it further onto the rocks it was already impaled upon. Erick frantically freed himself from the foremast rigging. Once again, he heard the sounds of wood being fractured and snapped as the rocky outcrop, in consort with the storm, continued to eviscerate the vessel's hull.

Erick made his way off the foredeck back to where he had watched the people through the dining salon window. He listened as one of the ship's officers, standing in the stairwell between decks, told one crewman, "Captain has given the order. Inform crew to gather passengers aft." Turning to a second crewman, he said, "You, take what men you need and make ready the four lifeboats and both surfboats. Captain's orders, we're to abandon ship." Erick watched as the second crewman, who couldn't have been much older than twenty-one, managed a salute despite his shaking hand, "Aye-aye Mr. Allen, sir." As the young crewman scurried to the rear of the ship, Mr. Allen turned towards Erick, "sir, you best heed all you've heard and be on your way." With a deep sigh, Mr. Allen shook his head and winced, "with these seas, we've nary the time to save but a few. God help us." As Mr. Allen entered the dining salon, Erick made his way to the lifeboats astern. He watched as the crew tried to launch one of the lifeboats at the rear of the ship. The first boat capsized, and everyone watched in horror as the waves sucked it beneath the stern. A second launch was attempted with a boat full of women, just behind the starboard paddlewheel, but a massive wave shattered the lifeboat against the side of the ship. First Officer Allen was fortunate to get all of the *women back aboard before the boat fell into the raging sea.*

A short time later, Erick watched Mr. Patterson lower a wooden surfboat containing five women, three children, ten crewmen as well as Mr. Patterson himself. Erick watched as the Third Mate and his crew successfully maneuvered the surfboat away from Brother Jonathan, disappearing into the heavy fog bank. As he stared into the water, he saw a woman treading water wearing two life preservers. Somewhere on deck, a woman screamed, "it's Mrs. Keenan... somebody do something!" But before a rescue attempt could be mounted, a wave lifted a large plank that had broken from the ship and brought it smashing down on her head. The woman's lifeless body drifted face down and out of view into the fog. As Brother Jonathan's stern began lifting up out of the sea, Erick saw the panic on the other passengers' faces. It was there that he saw the lovely woman standing with her husband and three young sons at the stern railing, all of them holding tightly to each other as the ship began to slide bow first into the frigid sea.

CHAPTER 3

(Tuesday Day 3 / October 13, 2020)

Erick awoke with a start, sitting straight up in bed. Gathering himself, he wiped the sleep from his eyes. Slinging the blankets off his legs, he pivoted, placing his feet on the floor. The memory of the dream was already fading, but it left him with an uneasy feeling that he could not shake. Getting out of bed, Erick made his way to the bathroom to begin his morning routine. While shaving, he mulled over the fragments he could recall from the dream. Then, like a candle being lit in a dark room, the light came on as it became apparent. It was the family assembled together at the railing just before the ship had gone down. The three boys standing with their parents at the barrier were the same three boys he had seen on the bench at the Bolen Annex. Then he had a second revelation, that particular thing he had picked up on but had been unable to pinpoint back at the annex. The boys in his dream were clothed precisely like the boys at the annex, and while dark wool pants with white long-sleeved shirts and leather ankle boots might have been fashionable for 1865, they were indeed out of date in the twenty-first century.

The smell of breakfast greeted Erick when he exited the bathroom. He finished dressing and retrieved his wallet and cellphone from the nightstand. Looking at his cellphone, he saw he had one unheard voicemail. Listening to the voicemail, he heard Richard, at Dick's Auto Repair, explaining that the part for his car was due to arrive this afternoon. Richard explained that barring any unforeseen hitches, he should have his Mercedes ready by five o'clock tomorrow. Richard had said if he could not pick it up to give him a call so he could move it to the garage before the storm made landfall tomorrow evening. Erick ended the call and returned his cellphone to his pocket before heading down to breakfast.

Shirley and Mabel were already eating when Erick stepped into the kitchen and said, good morning. He noticed a pair of paws poking out from under the table and knew it had to be Sir Barrymore Jr. patiently awaiting his morsels of bacon. The sisters greeted him with a good morning. Mabel said, "come on, sweetie, don't be shy, grab a seat and get ya some breakfast before it's all gone." Erick thanked her as he pulled a chair out. While fixing his plate, he asked Mabel if it was okay if he extended his stay another couple of days. He explained that Richard would not have his car ready until late tomorrow, and depending on the weather, he didn't know if he wanted to be on the road when the storm made landfall. Mabel was delighted, "oh Erick, you know you're welcome to stay as long as you need to." Shirley looked at Erick and gave him a lazy-eyed wink, "see there, we've grown on ya like a mushroom does a stump. Yep, you'll be hard-pressed to get rid of us now." Erick grinned and reached for the bowl of sausage gravy.

While they ate, Erick asked Shirley what she had meant about the reef being "cursed." She nodded her head, recalling their conversation, "yep, bad luck all around St. George Reef and that Lighthouse." Shirley went on to explain how men started losing their lives as soon as construction was underway. In June of 1891, a man fell to his death during construction. In April 1951, the reef claimed three more men when a rogue wave swamped a launch sending the men inside into the sea. "You been over to the park yet," Shirley asked? "No, I haven't had the opportunity yet," Erick said. Shirley told Erick he should see the park before the storm got much worse. That there were things over there, he needed to see. She explained how one of the biggest mysteries surrounding the St. George Reef Lighthouse occurred in October 1895. It involved the disappearance of a keeper. According to the lighthouse Board Report, the man left with the station boat and was never seen again. The man was presumed lost at sea. The entry read, "no remnant of man or vessel."

A grimace crept across Erick's face, "that's really odd. Nothing more?" "Nope," Shirley said, "They never got to the bottom of it apparently. I had a hard time finding out any more about it. I've heard tell one of the keepers was found in a pool of blood with his throat slit from here to here," Shirley made a slicing motion with her thumb from ear to ear." She explained that the three-man crew had been marooned on the reef by an unusually severe storm that had prevented their relief. The storm had been so intense that efforts to resupply had to be abandoned. When Men were able to reach the lighthouse, not a soul could be found; just a dead body and that haunting entry in the Board Report, "but that's the stuff of ghost stories. I haven't been able to confirm any of it."

After breakfast, Erick and Shirley sat at the table having coffee. Shirley tossed Sir Barrymore Jr. his bacon pieces while Erick recounted his dream. When he got to the end and described the family with the three boys astern at the ship's rail, Shirley stopped feeding Sir Barrymore Jr. and looked up, "what's that you say...three boys with their parents on deck at the rail?" Erick nodded and said, "yes." Shirley pushed back from the table and placed the plate of bacon on the floor. Standing up, she left the kitchen but on her way out said, "you stay put; I'll be back in a shake."

When she returned, she was holding the manila envelope from the night before, "look here, I'm fixin' to show you something that'll be hard to wrap your head around." Shirley pulled a piece of paper from the manila envelope and handed it to Erick, "what's this," he asked? Shirley nodded, "you go on and read that. It's an actual eyewitness account of one of the survivors, a Mary Tweedale Garretson; I came across it sometime back." Holding it, Erick saw the yellowish paper was an old photocopy of an even older article. The texture of the paper was brittle and stiff to the touch. On it was the faded yet readable image of the original article describing the eyewitness account of a Mary Tweedale regarding the last time she saw the Rowell family alive, "That sweet family, father, mother, standing on that pitching deck, their little ones clutching about them, the wind and spray lashing at their clothing, and she, that beautiful woman, gazing down at us so wistfully as we pulled away."

With a flat gaze, Erick sat in stunned silence. Thoughts swirled around in his head, causing him to grow nauseous from vertigo. He placed both hands on the table to steady himself. Shirley asked, "Erick, you okay?" Erick asked himself, was it even possible...how could he dream about a reality he had not seen or heard of before? Perhaps the Rowell family was mentioned in the Brother Jonathan exhibit at the annex; had he read about it and simply forgotten? With concern on her face, Shirley pressed, "Say something." But how could I forget something like that when I remember everything else about that day? No, that's just not possible; I would've remembered something like this. Erick felt a warm hand squeezing his shoulder. He looked to his right to see Shirley, her eyebrows drawn together, and her lips pursed, staring intensely into his eyes. In a deep voice, she said, "you with me? While you were reading the article, your face went all white, and you wouldn't answer me. Are you okay, hun?" Erick played it off and told her he thought the stress was getting to him. With his father's death and all, he had been under a tremendous amount of stress. His car trouble and the approaching storm only compounded matters. He assured Shirley there had to be a logical explanation for all of this. Erick noticed that Mabel had stopped doing the dishes and was staring at him with a concerned look on her face. Even Sir Barrymore Jr. was staring at him with a curious look on his face, though Bear-Bear was more likely wondering if this meant more bacon bits. Erick smiled a reassuring smile, "really, ladies, don't worry about me. I'm fine." After thanking Mabel for another great breakfast, he excused himself. He told the sisters he had something to take care of in town and would return around lunchtime.

Erick left Aunt Mabel's and drove straight to the Bolen Annex over on H Street behind the Del Norte County Historical Society Museum. He parked along the curb line and exited his car. The wind had really picked up again, and the temperature had markedly dropped, which made the light drizzle all the more unpleasant. He made his way to the front door of the annex and peeked through the window. With a cursory glance, everything looked as it had on his last visit; surely, the sisters were mistaken; the museum had simply reopened without their knowledge. Grabbing hold of the knob, he gave it a twist, and the door swung open. Dust particles floated in the beams of sunlight streaming through the large windows. Erick crossed the room to where the Brother Jonathan exhibit was located. He could see the massive ship's wheel, and...sure enough, seated at the wooden bench were the three young boys from the other day. Studying the boys, Erick was confident they were the same boys from his dream; they were even wearing the same clothes. The boys sat in complete silence, staring at him. He smiled and nodded his head as if to say hello, but they didn't acknowledge him. Again, Erick had the uneasy feeling they were staring right through him. He concluded enough was enough and decided to introduce himself. As he started to walk in their direction, he heard the curator, Mr. Duffy, from behind, "Mr. Williamson! Yer a sight fer sore eyes. Welcome back, lad!" Erick turned around and saw Mr. Duffy in full regalia, with both fists on his hips like *Yul Brynner* from the movie *The King and I*. Erick asked Mr. Duffy if he had some time to spare so he could ask him some questions? The curator stroked his wiry beard and raises an eyebrow and said, "I'll answer if I'm able, ask away." Erick asked about the three boys seated on the bench. "Ah, that's easy enough. They be Daniel and Polina's, lads. Let's see, there's Elias...Henry... Charles...and young Paul." Mr. Duffy grins and shakes his head, "that young Paul has itchy feet. The lad likes to wander off, but he's about somewhere." No sooner had Mr. Duffy mentioned the youngest boy's name when Erick heard the eerie echo of a child's giggles from somewhere amongst the dusty exhibits. Turning to ascertain the giggles' direction, Erick noticed the three boys were missing from their bench. He hurried over to the wooden bench and looked around the corner and down the aisle, but there was no sign the boys had ever been there. Again, the giggles echoed throughout the building as a boom of thunder crashed, reverberating throughout the annex. The lights inside the building flickered before going out entirely. Erick heard the rain hitting the roof as the light drizzle outside turned to a steady downpour. Mr. Duffy walked over to where Erick was standing by the Brother Jonathan exhibit and asked, "what's the matter, lad?" Erick turned towards the curator just as a flash of lightning illuminated the interior of the annex. The lightning flashed across the curator's face revealing his maniacal grin, "ya don't mind my sayin', ya look as if ya seen a ghost!"

When Erick woke, he was sitting in the rental car parked outside the Bolen Annex. He had no recollection of how he made it back to the car or how long he had been unconscious. For a minute, he even entertained the possibility that he had not yet gone in, that he had dozed off and dreamt the bizarre encounter. But that didn't make any sense because his clothes were soaking wet. From the shelter of the car, Erick stared through the rain blurred window. He could see the interior of the annex was dark. Exiting the vehicle, he made his way to the front door of the annex. He needed to speak with Mr. Duffy if for no other reason than to satisfy his curiosity.

Erick yanked his coat tightly around his body, hoping to retain as much warmth as possible. The current weather conditions were more befitting the type of storm the meteorologist had all been hyping. Erick reached down and took hold of the doorknob. He turned the knob, but nothing happened. He jiggled it several more times, but there was no use; the door was locked. He moved to one of the large side windows. Like a kid in front of a toy store, Erick peered through the glass with cupped hands. The interior was dark except for the illumination provided by the occasional flash of lightning. As far as he could tell, everything looked as it had. Nothing appeared strange or out of the ordinary. He was just about to turn and head back to the car when he noticed the footprints. Wet footprints were leading from the front door over to the staircase. Erick assumed the prints ascended the stairs since that's where the last discernable print was pointed. He also knew they weren't his footprints. Firstly, because he hadn't gone near the stairs when he had been inside earlier, and secondly, these footprints were larger than any he might have made. These prints looked as if they had been made by someone wearing clunky galoshes. Erick decided he had seen enough. Wet, cold, and more than a little confused, he returned to the car.

As he drove back to Aunt Mabel's, Erick considered how best to explain his latest adventure in bizarroland. He thought of different ways to word the experience. Still, no matter how he described it, he realized he would come off as a lunatic. Making his way down Ninth Street, the car radio came to life with a piercing shriek that snapped Erick from his thoughts. The alert tone was followed by the voice of a man, "This is a test of the Emergency Alert System. In cooperation with federal, state, and local authorities, the broadcasters have developed this system to keep you informed in the event of an emergency. If this had been an actual emergency, the Attention Signal you just heard would have been followed by official information, news, or instructions. This concludes this test of the Emergency Alert System serving the coastal areas of Del Norte and Humboldt counties in northern California." Erick thought, if the authorities are testing the Emergency Alert System, it's a safe bet the storm has intensified. He made his way past the school and through the intersection of Ninth and E Streets. He was grateful to find the city had managed to solve the drainage situation.

Erick pulled along the curb in front of Aunt Mabel's and parked. Sitting in the car, he noted that since he had left the annex, the weather had only intensified. Exiting the car, he turned to the left, closing the door behind him. This time, as he pauses at the trunk staring at the pooled water, he simply trudged right through it like a two-year-old playing in a puddle. Mounting the curb, he looked up and saw Mabel and Shirley standing at the bay window applauding and laughing. Even Sir Barrymore Jr. approved; Erick could see the little dog yapping at the bay window from one of the wingbacks. Like a triumphant gymnast having just stuck the landing, he clicked his heels together, extended his arms, and thrust his nose up into the air. Both sisters continued laughing and started waving for him to come inside.

Shirley was sitting in the living room with a cup of coffee watching the latest news on the approaching storm, and Mabel had wandered off to the kitchen. Shirley told Erick the weather forecast wasn't great; the predictions had reported the storm was rapidly strengthening and still moving in a southeasterly direction. Nodding at the television, Shirley said, "Redwood Weather Authority is saying landfall around early evening tomorrow and will most likely—." "Clobber us head-on! That is what they're all saying. You may as well call it like it is Shirl," Mabel cut in, returning to the room with a cup of coffee for Erick. Taking the cup of coffee, Erick could sense the tension in Mabel's voice. That she had cut Shirley off midsentence wasn't lost on him either; that was entirely out of character for Mabel. He knew she hadn't intended on being rude to Shirley; she was just nervous and concerned. Erick watched as Mabel sat down on the sofa and turned, giving the television her undivided attention. Shirley glanced at Erick with raised eyebrows and a pressed, tight-lipped smile before turning back to Mabel, "now, Mabel, you know there's nothing to fret about; we've been through worse." Shirley explained how she had been in Miami when Hurricane Donna hit the Florida Keys as a category four back in 1960. Next, she reminded Mabel of Camille hitting the Mississippi coast as a category five back in '69. Then there had been Hugo and Andrew, both category fours in '89 and '92, respectively. "Hugo made landfall around Charleston, South Carolina. Andrew hit South Florida as a four before running across the Gulf and slamming into the Louisiana coast as a three," Shirley added as she walked over and turned the television off. Noticeably perturbed, Mabel said, "Why'd ya do that, Shirley? I was watching that." "Because Mabel, it's only upsetting you. Besides, you know all there is to know for now. Best leave it be, can't do anything about it anyway," Shirley said as a matter of fact, "besides, don't you wanna hear what Erick has been up to." Though she wasn't pleased with Shirley, Mabel turned to face Erick and donned a smile, "of course I wanna hear about his day. Erick, sweetheart, you go right ahead."

Erick went over and took a seat by the bay window. He stared for a moment at the sisters who were seated side by side on the sofa. Replaying the encounter repeatedly in his head, he realized there was no way to explain it in which he didn't sound crazy. He concluded to tell the story as it happened and let the chips fall where they may. And so, after a deep breath, Erick explained his latest encounter with curator Duffy and the three boys on the bench at the Bolen Annex.

When he had finished, there was a long pause. Mabel excused herself and left for the kitchen to start preparing dinner. Shirley was the first to break the silence, "so this curator not only told you the names of the three boys, but he also said they were the sons of Daniel and Polina Rowell?" Erick nodded, "that's what he said." Shirley leaned back into the sofa cushions and removed her eyeglasses. Erick could tell something was on her mind, something she wanted to ask him but wasn't sure how to word. She began rubbing her eyes with her forefinger and thumb. Taking a deep breath and hanging her spectacles back on the bridge of her nose, she asked, "did he, by chance, mention a fourth child?" "What makes you ask that?" Erick said, "I've never mentioned anything about there being a fourth boy." Erick's evasiveness was transparent, but he didn't want to try and explain the little boy's phantom giggles to Shirley. He wasn't even sure he believed that part of the story himself. Up until now, he had been able to rationalize everything. Still, ghostly giggles was a bridge he found difficult to cross. Shirley pushed her glasses up with her forefinger. Leaning in, she asked, "who mentioned anything about the fourth child being a boy?" growing impatient, Shirley stared intently at Erick, "look here, stop beatin' round the bush. Come clean." Erick finally admitted Duffy had mentioned a fourth child named Paul. Reluctantly, Erick also recounted the unsettling giggles he had heard as soon as the name had been said. He even told Shirley about the lightning knocking the lights out and how Duffy had acted bizarre, telling Erick, "ya look as if ya seen a ghost." After some thought, Shirley said, "as I recall, you never did answer that question back when I asked." Erick said, "at that time, I didn't, but a lot has happened since then. Now..." he began shaking his head, "...now I don't know what to believe." Shirley asked Erick if he had been to the park across the street yet, and he explained that he hadn't yet had the opportunity. Shirley said, "I think it's about time you visit the park, Erick. I reckon there are answers over there for questions you haven't begun to ask yet." Shirley tilted her head towards the kitchen where her nose had picked-up the aroma of supper, "oh my, we're in for a real treat. Smells like Mabel is about to serve up some of her famous homemade stuffin' patties. Normally she only makes those on Thanksgiving. I reckon she's practicing for next month."

After supper, Erick excused himself and made an early night of it. He would be picking-up his Mercedes tomorrow evening from Dick's Auto Repair and wanted to get some sleep. He would need to be well-rested for the long drive home. He had enjoyed his stay at Aunt Mabel's B&B and had grown quite fond of the sisters... including Sir Barrymore Jr., but it was time he got back to his life in the real world. It was time to lay his father to rest, closing this chapter of his life and starting anew.

CHAPTER 4

(Wednesday Day 4 / October 14, 2020)

Erick couldn't tell what, or even if anything had roused him from sleep when he first opened his eyes. The room was pitch black except for the streetlight's dingy orange glow shining through the bedroom window from across the street. A flash of lightning abruptly lit the room. Erick began counting, "one Mississippi, two Mississippi, three Mississippi, four Missis—." A low rumble reverberated through the room. Reaching for his cellphone on the nightstand to check the time, he inadvertently knocks his wallet and keys to the floor. Erick read the lock screen on his cellphone and saw it was two-twenty-five in the morning. He put his cellphone back on the nightstand and made a mental note that his wallet and keys were somewhere on the floor.

As Erick was drifting back to sleep, a flash of lightning bathed the room in bright light. He was about to start counting when he heard the giggles of a child coming from what sounded like just outside the window. A deep growl of thunder rolled in the distance as he peeled back the blankets and walked over to the window. Staring out across the foggy street, his eyes were drawn to movement over by the park. Sometime during the night, a thick fog had settled over the park. Still, Erick could just make out the figure of a young child. The child appeared to be about four or five. Erick watched as the little one ran around a circular formation of white stones positioned around a flagpole. An icy chill ran down the nape of his neck when the child stopped, turned, and gazed up at him, and began giggling. As bizarre and disturbing as it was, Erick was not about to let superstitious fantasies of the supernatural override his concern for this child's safety. Sliding his slippers onto his feet, he grabbed his nightrobe and headed down the stairs for the front door.

Erick walked across the street and mounted the sidewalk next to the park proper. The thick fog made it difficult to see very far at ground level. Though the heavy rain from earlier had tapered off to a steady drizzle, the wind was still wintery cold. To the northwest, out over the Pacific, Erick could see the approaching storm. He watched the dark, ominous clouds throw off sporadic bursts of lightning. Stepping onto the grass of the park, he cringed, muttering an expletive under his breath, as his foot sank into the muddy morass created by all the rain. Erick walked towards the flagpole through the fog where he had last seen the child from his bedroom window. When he reached the circle, he realized they were not just stones but rather gravestones that had been laid flat. Bending down to get a closer look, he heard the child giggle again, this time off to his right.

Quickly looking to his right, he caught a glimpse of the child's white gown as it disappeared behind a large object. From its silhouette, the large item seemed to be a boulder or stone of some sort. Flanking the large boulder, Erick could discern a pair of large ship's anchors from their distinct profiles. He called to the child but only got more giggles coming from behind the boulder. Erick sloshed up to the boulder and placed a steadying hand on the cold stone, "okay, kid, the gig's up; I found you." Slowly, he leaned around the side of the boulder, but to his astonishment, no child was standing there. No child, no dress, not even footprints to indicate there had ever been a child standing there. Standing next to the boulder, Erick saw a large plaque affixed to it. He strained to read the inscription, but it was pointless; there was simply not enough light. As he chided himself for not having the presence of mind to grab his cellphone, he heard more giggling. This time from behind, in the direction of S Pebble Beach Drive. Spinning, Erick placed his back against the cold boulder.

Across the park, beyond the dingy hue cast by the streetlight lighting the street, Erick strained to see through the darkness at the other side of the roadway. Crossing the road, he entered the small parking lot. Walking to the edge of the bluff, he stood at the metal guiderail and stared down into the blackness below. He listened as the sea hurled itself against the rocks. Like smoke on a battlefield, the briny mist rose up. He could feel it on his face and tasted the salt on his lips. Rising with the mist was the faint sound of the child's giggles interwoven with the ruckus raging below. Even though it made no sense, Erick could not deny what his ears were hearing. As he listened, the giggles seemed to take on an almost mocking characteristic before they gradually drifted off out over the water and faded away. Chilled to the bone and more than a little disconcerted, Erick mumbled, "are you kidding me...I mean, what the...I must be losing it?" In the end, he decided it was best to simply return to Aunt Mabel's and salvage what sleep he could before sunrise.

Not even the smell of Mabel's country breakfast was enough to ease the raw, edgy feeling that Erick was experiencing when he awoke. What little sleep he had managed had been shallow and restless at best. Wiping the sleep from his eyes, he began to question his memory of the events from the early morning hours. In the light of day, the whole thing seemed so surreal as to be unbelievable. He was beginning to question if any of it had even taken place. Was it possible he had dreamed one of those really vivid dreams that people mistake for reality? Any doubts he might have had were quickly laid to rest when he placed his feet on the floor and saw his muddy slippers next to the nightstand beside his keys and wallet.

After a quick shower and shave, he put some clothes

on and went downstairs for breakfast. Coming down the stairs, he noticed the television was tuned to the Weather Authority, where the news was updating the approaching storm's status. The sisters were in the kitchen having breakfast and discussing the latest news updates. "Morning Erick, grab a seat and have some breakfast," Mabel said. Shirley looked up and said, "good morning. Hope you're hungry." Erick smiled and said, "good morning, ladies." Taking a seat, he apologized for any mud he might have tracked into the house during his early morning escapades. Mabel said, "nope, not a smudge. Must've given them a good wipe on the mat before coming back in." Shirley spoke up, "I thought I heard the door close a couple of times this morning. Wasn't sure if it was Mabel or a ghost. Bear-Bear didn't fret it, so I let it slide."

While they ate breakfast, Erick explained his reason for leaving the house at such an unusual hour. He described how he had followed the child through the park and eventually across the street to the parking lot, where the child mysteriously vanished into thin air. Erick looked up and gave an uneasy grin, "you know, for a minute there, when I was standing by the guiderail, I could've sworn the kid was taunting me...but that's crazy, right?" When he had finished, Mabel jumped up and took her plate to the sink. Leaning against the edge of the sink with both palms, Mabel stared at the sink full of soap suds, "Shirley Dean, it's time. One of us needs to tell him." Erick looked at Mabel and then Shirley, "tell me what? What is it the two of you have been so reticent to share?" "Shirley, if you don't, I will, I mean it..." Mabel said more firmly, "Erick, did you notice the white stones last night when you were in the park?" "Yes, I saw the ring of white stones going around the flagpole. They looked to be part of a memorial of some sorts, but what does that have to do with anything?"

Shirley leaned back in her chair and tore off another piece of bacon, tossing it to Sir Barrymore Jr. under the table, "go on, Erick, grab your jacket. You and I can talk about this in the truck." Getting up from the table, Shirley continued, "Mabel, we'll be back shortly. Need to grab a few things from the Home Depot before this storm gets here. We'll run by the Grocery Outlet as well. Is there anything I need to add to my list?" Turning her back to the sink, Mabel said, "Nope, nothing I can think of off the top of my head. You two take care; weather's gonna get nasty. Be sure to give my love to Gigi." Leaving the kitchen, Shirley said, "We will. Bear-bear stay...Erick come-on."

Erick retrieved his jacket and met Shirley out at the truck idling in the driveway. There was a steady drizzle but no real rain. Erick climbed into the cab of the 1972 Chevrolet pickup, "okay," Erick asked, "before we get started, what's up with the color?" Leaning forward with her hands at the top of the wheel, Shirley tilted her head to look at Erick, "what you mean? The aqua blue exterior or the orange leather seats?" Erick grinned, "all of it. What am I missing?" Shirley shook her head, "this is my baby," she said, rubbing the dashboard with her hand, "come on, Erick, you can't figure it out?...' 72 Chevy done up in aqua blue and orange?" Erick just stared at her. "Really?... I bet I could give you two nickels for a dime, and you'd think you were rich." Shirley let out a howl and said, "Lord have mercy! Dolphins Erick...More specifically, the perfect 1972 Miami Dolphins that went 14-0! C'mon, son, you gotta be quicker on the draw than that." Erick shrugged and said, "oh, okay." Shirley shook her head and pulled out of the driveway, making a left onto Ninth Street, "guess you're not a big football fan. Well, suppose every dog should have a few fleas," she laughed.

As they drove through town on their way to the Home Depot, Shirley asked, "heard you say you saw the white stones last night. Any chance you read what was on any of 'em?" Erick shook his head, "no, it was too dark." Shirley just nodded her head and kept driving. "you were partly right; it is a memorial, in a way." She paused and brought the truck to a stop at a red light before turning to face Erick, "truth be told, it's a cemetery. Before that was ever the Brother Jonathan Park Memorial, it was first the old Pioneer or Masonic Cemetery." Lost in thought, Shirley continued, "no, sir, you're not the first person to see something over there they couldn't explain, and I'd be willing to bet the farm you ain't gonna be the last neither." Car horns began blaring from behind. Shirley leaned forward and looked up at the traffic light, "I see...I see, y'all hold your horses." As they pulled through the intersection and continued on, Erick let out a nervous chuckle, "so what you're saying is that I was chasing the ghost—, no, no, no...wait. That

I was running around in a cemetery at two o'clock in the morning; in my pajamas, nonetheless. Playing hide-and-seek with the ghost of some child?" Shirley turned and leaned her head to one side and winked, "just remember, you said it, not me." Erick sat in silence for the rest of the trip to the Home Depot. His mind kept mulling everything over as he reevaluated and considered all he had experienced. It's one big oxymoron, he thought; the one thing that makes sense of everything is the very thing that makes no sense at all, that being this notion that ghosts are somehow real.

As they pulled into the Home Depot parking lot, they were surprised by how few cars were in the lot. Shirley let out a long sigh, "Oh my, looks like we may be a day late and a dollar short. I hope they still have what we need. Tell you what, let's kill two birds with one stone, run grab one of them orange doohickies off yonder and meet me inside by the plywood." A couple of flashes of lightning arced across the sky right as they exited the truck. Shirley made her way to the front of the store while Erick retrieved one of the orange metal utility carts. As he maneuvered the awkward cart through the parking lot, he could see evidence that the wind was beginning to pick up as a plastic bag raced across the lot before jumping into the air. Erick watched as the bag floated up into the sky like a child's lost balloon at an amusement park. Somewhat mesmerized by the bag floating off, his daydream was interrupted as the drizzle turned to a downpour.

Erick entered the Home Depot and headed straight

to the section where the lumber was kept. He found Shirley halfway down aisle #9, inspecting what was left of the plywood. A young man in an orange apron was standing next to her. Shirley had her left arm folded across her abdomen and her right hand under her chin as she shook her head from side-to-side. Based on the look on her face, Erick surmised it wasn't good news. "So, this is all y'all have left? You don't have any more of that strengthened plywood?" The young man shook his head, "no, ma'am, this is all that's left in the city. We should be getting some more in by next week if you want to stop back by." The young man realized what he had said only after the words had left his mouth. Shirley tilted her head and shot Erick a raised eyebrow before refocusing her glare back to the young man. Feeling somewhat sorry for the young associate Erick stepped in and asked Shirley if she couldn't somehow use what they had? Shirley looked at Erick, "Don't see that we have much choice. Not unless this fella here can coax the storm into a time-out for a week or so until they get another load in." Erick thanked the young employee for his help, and the young man gratefully disappeared down another aisle. Erick asked Shirley how many boards they needed? "Ten boards should do it. I have a circular saw in the garage. We can cut them to size," she said, as she dropped two boxes of screws onto the orange cart before continuing, "grabbed a couple boxes of three-inch lag screws to secure 'em to the window frames with." Erick and Shirley rolled the cart to the check-out stand and paid for their items. After paying for everything, they pushed the cart into the entry/

exit bay and took stock of the situation. Shirley's eyes widened like saucers, "Lord have mercy, it's blowin' up a storm out there!" Erick had to admit, the storm had intensified in the short time they had been inside the store. Erick and Shirley buttoned up their jackets and pulled their collars up in preparation for the onslaught they knew awaited them as soon as they left the shelter of the store's bay. With the plywood loaded in the truck's bed, Shirley and Erick sat in the truck with the heater running, trying to warm up. A few minutes later, Shirley turned the heater down and said, "best run over to the Grocery Outlet before it gets much worse."

On their way to the Grocery Outlet, they drove by the Safeway. Shirley nodded at the parking lot and said, "that right there is the reason we're going to the Grocery Outlet over on Third Street; I figured folks would take leave of their senses. There'll be less chance of these shenanigans at the Outlet." As they drove by, Erick could see people running around in a panic all over the place. There were so many people trying to get into the parking lot that cars had formed a log jam at the parking lot entrance causing a backup that stretched all the way from N Street out to Fifth Street. The whole scene was reminiscent of an old photo he recalled from a history book back in high school. Erick remembered how they had been studying the great gasoline shortages of the 1970s. In the photo, you could see people waiting outside their cars in front of gas stations in lines reaching as far back as the eye could see.

Shirley continued past the Safeway and made a right

onto Third Street. after a block, she made another right. They pulled into the Grocery Outlet parking lot. At the Grocery Outlet, everything appeared to be business as usual. Shirley pulled into an empty stall and turned off the engine. Erick noted the look of satisfaction on Shirley's face as she pulled the keys from the ignition. Clearly reveling in her ability to predict herd mentality in a crisis situation. "I've never been one to say I told ya so, but..." She left the comment hanging like a backdoor screen with a broken spring as she stepped out of the truck.

Except for a pair of teenage skateboarders milling about, the store parking lot was a ghost town. As they were entering the store, one of the skateboarders, a redheaded boy, asked Erick for the time. Checking his watch, Erick told the young man it was almost two o'clock. "Thanks, man," the redheaded boy said. Turning to his partner, a taller young man wearing a pinstripe hat with the word "Reckless" emblazoned in red across the front, the redheaded boy said, "yo! Tristan, it's almost two. I need to scoot, or my dad is gonna be pissed." The boy in the "Reckless" hat nodded his head upwards and responded, "right on, Justin. I'm chillin' until this rain lets up before I head out. Catch you later, bro."

Shirley and Erick entered the Grocery store and were greeted by a tall redheaded woman dressed in a Grocery Outlet uniform. Erick watched as the redhead and Shirley exchange a hug before Shirley turned to introduce her, "Erick, this is Virginia Ann or 'Gigi' as Mabel, and I like to call her." Turning to Virginia, Shirley says, "Gigi, this is Erick Williamson. He's been our lodger since Sunday." Virginia shifted a pack of Winston cigarettes from her right to left hand. She smiled and reached out her right arm to shake hands, "pleased to meet you, Mr. Williamson, though I wish it were under better circumstances." Shaking her hand, Erick smiled and said, "the pleasure is all mine, and please call me Erick." Virginia nodded and smiled, "well, in that case, feel free to call me 'Gigi.' After all, any friend of Mabel and Shirley is undoubtedly a friend of mine." Having just met the woman, Erick couldn't explain why, but he really liked this "Gigi." There was just something about her that told him she was someone you could trust. He felt she was cut from the same cloth as Mabel and Shirley, a kindred spirit.

As the three of them stood at the far end of the checkout lanes, Gigi drew closer to Shirley. She explained that she had been on a cigarette break talking with her sister Sue on her cellphone before they had pulled up. Apparently, Sue was a checker over at the Safeway they had passed on their way to the Grocery Outlet. Gigi explained that Sue had said it was a complete madhouse over there. Sue related how the manager had to call the police because of fights breaking out over toilet paper rolls. Gigi shook her head in disbelief, "toilet paper Shirley? Tell me, does that not take the cake?" Shirley started shaking her head in disgust, "yeah, we drove by Safeway on our way here. Seems like the closer this storm gets, the more folks take leave of their senses.

Y'all best close down and board up before the circus comes to town over here." Nodding in agreement, Gigi said, "you two best get what you need while you still can." Gigi gave Shirley another hug and winked at Erick from over Shirley's shoulder. Erick smiled back and then chased after Shirley.

Shirley had grabbed a shopping cart and was methodically working her way down the aisles. She knew exactly what they needed and precisely where to find it. Having mostly filled their cart with water, rice, beans, and various canned goods, they began working their way towards the checkout lanes. Shirley and Erick stood there trying to figure out which line was moving the fastest when out of the blue, a lady grabbed the front of their cart, pulling the handle right out of Shirley's hands. Before Erick could protest, he noticed the uniform and flaming red hair; it was Gigi to their rescue, he thought. Gigi and Shirley continued their talk while Gigi scanned their groceries. As the two women spoke, Erick's attention was drawn to the commotion taking place out in the parking lot, just on the other side of the large windows. Erick could see Tristan had his cellphone out and was holding it up, recording something. Erick saw two women at the center of all the commotion, a brunette, and a blonde, engaged in a fistfight. Erick watched speechless as the brunette grabbed a handful of the blondes' hair and began dragging her around by the head of her hair while simultaneously punching the blonde about the head and face. Though she was trying, the blonde woman was unable to get to her feet. The best the blonde could do was hold onto the hand that had hold of her hair with one hand and fend off the blows with the other. Erick couldn't tell if the two men halfheartedly attempting to separate the women were their husbands or boyfriends. Still, it was apparent the women were having none of it. Erick felt empathy for the two men. He could tell from the looks on their faces that this was not their first rodeo. They had both been down this sordid road with their significant others in the past.

Hearing Gigi ring-up the total, Erick turned his attention back to the matter at hand. Shirley pushed the cart of bagged groceries forward, handing the cart off to Erick. While she paid Gigi for the groceries, Shirley said, "Virginia Ann, Mabel sends her love. You come by and have some supper real soon. We miss you, girl." Gigi smiled and sent her love to Mabel. She also promised to come by as soon as she was able. Leaving the store, Erick and Shirley paused under the store's overhang to button up their jackets before heading out into the wind and rain. Erick looked over at Tristan, who was still recording the two women fighting. Tristan glanced at Erick with a mischievous grin on his face and said, "you gotta capture life's moments' man." Erick shook his head, "shouldn't you be home instead of out here in the middle of all of this?" Tristan just shrugged and laughed, "this is some gnarly footage. YouTube gold right here, dude. Jerry Springer, eat your heart out!" Erick just shook his head and trailed after Shirley through the parking lot. Once everything was loaded, they hopped in and got the engine going. Exiting the parking lot, Shirley told Erick, "now the real fun begins. We still need to prepare the house before this storm makes landfall later tonight."

By the time Shirley and Erick returned, Mabel had pulled the BBQ grill and all of the backyard lawn furniture into the garage. Turning on to the driveway, they could see her bent over at the side of the house, reeling the garden hose onto the hose caddy. Hearing the truck, Mabel looked up and waved at them with her free hand as they pulled up the driveway. Though they both saw it, neither was in a position to prevent what happened next. One of the massive tree branches belonging to the old Oregon Oak, the one Shirley had warned Mabel about just last year, buckled and snapped under the intensity of the ever-increasing winds. They both watched in dread as the enormous bough fell some twenty feet before striking Mabel and knocking her to the concrete driveway. Shirley slammed on the breaks, coming to a screeching stop, and threw the truck into park as they both kicked their doors open and raced down the driveway. "Mabel!-oh my Lord-please, no-Mabel!" Shirley shouted as they made their way to where the hulking branch had landed. As soon as they arrived at the pile of debris, Erick heard the frantic yapping of Sir Barrymore Jr. coming from the backyard. No doubt the little poodle had alerted to the urgency in Shirley's voice and was coming to see what the matter was. Erick watched as the little dog came tearing around the corner of the house. Before Shirley could get there, the little dog had dove headfirst into the debris of branches and limbs. Frantically barking, the little dog was conducting his own search and rescue for Mabel. Somehow, amid all the confusion, Erick was able to make out a pitifully faint whisper of a voice from beneath all the mangled branches, "Shirley...Shirley...Shirley." Each time the name was spoken just a little louder than before. Shirley yelled, "Mabel! Where are you, honey! I can't see you; where are you?" Then the faint voice again, "Shirley...please get Bear-Bear off me." Shirley grabbed the little dog, and Erick waded into the maze of branches, removing them one by one, revealing where Mabel had been pinned. Erick reached down, helping her back to her feet, and gave her a cursory once-over. He assisted her as she gingerly made her way out of the jungle of fallen foliage over to where Shirley stood, praising Sir Barrymore Jr. for saving Mabel's life. From what he could tell, except for a knot on the head and a scrape on her chin, she appeared no worse for wear. Given the circumstances, it could have been much worse, he thought. After helping Mabel to the living room sofa, Erick returned to the truck and began unloading the groceries and supplies in the truck bed.

After unloading the truck, Erick joined the sisters in the living room. The sisters were glued to the television, which was tuned to the Redwood News Weather Authority. Erick stood at the end of the coffee table and listened as the meteorologist gave the most current update on the approaching storm,

"The National Weather Service has issued a significant high-wind warning for Coos, Curry and Del Norte counties. The warning will be in effect from Wednesday evening until early Friday morning. Weather service models predict sustained winds of 60 to 70 miles per hour, with gusts that could potentially hit hurricane force. Ladies and gentlemen, we're talking gusts that could reach upwards of 120 to 150 miles per hour along the headlands and other exposed areas. Our coastal waters can expect hurricane-force gusts and dangerous seas. The winds will initially be southerly but will switch to northerly as the low passes. As we said in the morning broadcast, the National Weather Service describes this system as a rapidly deepening 'bomb' cyclone. We can't emphasize how important it is to be prepared and find suitable shelter from this storm. Please stay tuned to Redwood News for further updates as this story continues to develop. Remember, the Weather Authority is your authority on the weather when it happens and when it matters."

After the Weather report, Shirley said, "Mabel, you stay put right here on the sofa with Sir Barrymore Jr. while Erick and I batten down the hatches and trim the sails." Looking at Erick, Shirley asked, "look, I know you wanted to head over to Dick's today, but...well, boarding these windows would be a two-man job in the best of conditions. I sure could use an extra pair of hands...?" Erick feigned a look of hurt, "why Shirley, I thought you knew me better by now. I couldn't go anywhere without first knowing the two of you were safe and sound." Mabel looked at Erick and then at Shirley, "I told you,

Shirley, he belongs here. I felt it that first day. There's just something about him. He has an old soul."

Despite the rain and windy conditions, Erick and Shirley worked their way around the house, boarding the windows with plywood. From the top of the ladder, Erick could see over the backyard shrubs and, for the first time, was able to glimpse what everyone was so concerned about. He had never seen anything like it before in his life. It looked like a special effects scene generated by a CGI company for one of those apocalyptic movies Hollywood was so fond of putting out. The storm system was massive. The strange thing about it was, from that distance, at least, it didn't look all that destructive. As a matter of fact, the clouds didn't appear to be moving at all. *Ah, but that was the rub. After all,* he thought, *this was precisely why you couldn't always trust what you saw with your eyes because the eyes often lied.* Deep down, he knew the truth; behind that calm veneer lurked a menacing force waiting to unleash all manner of destruction. "First time seeing one?" Shirley said from inside the second-floor window. Erick nodded his head. Shirley glared out at the approaching cyclone, "yes sir, forces of nature are a mighty powerful sight to behold, even beautiful in some respects, no doubt 'bout that." Her eyes narrowed as she continued, "but it only looks that way. You familiar with the term 'the calm before the storm?' Make no mistake, son, that there's a killer." With apprehension, the two of them watched a little longer before finally getting back to the task at hand.

After they had finished boarding all of the windows, Erick told the sisters he was heading over to Dick's to see if his car was ready. He asked if there was anything they needed him to pick up while he was out, but they just shook their heads and said they'd be fine. As he grabbed his jacket and keys, Mabel walked over to give him a hug and whispered, "you watch yourself, you hear?" Erick smiled and said, "I sure will. You two stay dry. I'll see you soon." From over on the couch, Shirley rolled her eyes, "Enough, you two. Erick, best get to getting so you can beat that storm back." Closing the front door, as he stepped onto the porch, he could hear Sir Barrymore Jr. yapping before Shirley said, "Bear-Bear, you hush. My goodness, but you two act like he ain't ever comin' back." With that, Erick jumped from the porch and sprinted through the rain to the rental car.

Erick sat in the rental car, waiting for the engine to warm. As he waited, he gazed over at the Brother Jonathan Park cemetery. Once the heater began to circulate warm air, he shifted the car into drive. Instead of making a U-turn and heading towards Dick's Auto Repair, he drove straight towards S Pebble Beach Drive. When he got to the intersection, he glanced back over at the park and decided that he may as well check it out since he was there. He drove across the street and parked in the parking lot where the giggling ghost of a kid had taunted him. He parked the car and got out. He could hear the waves crashing against the rocks below, only this time no giggles were teasing him. Pelted by the rain and wind, Erick tugged his jacket tightly around his body. He pulled his collar up against the wind as he crossed the street and entered the cemetery. He made his way towards the large boulder flanked by the two large anchors. Standing there in the pouring rain and lashing wind, he read the inscription on the plaque affixed to the rock:

"Brother Jonathan Cemetery. This memorial is dedicated to those who lost their lives in the wreck of the Pacific mail steamer BROTHER JONATHAN, at Point St. George Reef. July 30, 1865."

Further on, Erick saw a walkway extending east towards a ring of stones. These must be the stones the sisters had insisted he see, he thought. He walked over to the markers and began reading the epitaphs one by one. He noticed all of the ones for those who perished aboard Brother Jonathan shared the same general epitaph. The only difference, of course, was the names and ages of the decedents. As he walked the ring reading the markers, he came across one that caused him to pause. The stone read, "Polna Rowell Drowned at the wreck of the Brother Jonathan July 30, 1865, aged 22 ys 6 ms & 7 days." The name was familiar to Erick, but he was having trouble placing it.

As he continued his walk among the stones, he came to a second one that sounded familiar. The inscription read, "Daniel C. Rowell Drowned at the wreck of the Brother Jonathan July 30, 1865, aged 38 ys 6 ms & 17 days." Erick stood in front of the stone deep in thought, doing his best to recall why the names were familiar to him. The wind had really picked up and was blowing the rain so hard that it stung when it struck the exposed skin of his face. What was it that Duffy had told him, " ah yes, they'd be Daniel and Polina's, lads." Erick rolled the names around in his head like a pair of dice, "Daniel and Polina, Daniel and Polna, Polina, Polna!" He stood there in the downpour, shaking his head, "this made no sense. It was impossible. These people had died in 1865 for crying out loud." He tried to reason it all away, "I must be out of my mind to even entertain such a possibility." He continued walking until he reached the easternmost section of the formation. There he saw a wooden structure with an eave. Beneath the eave was an information board that displayed numerous plaques. At the very top of the board, a plaque read, "Brother Jonathan Cemetery." There were several smaller plaques on the board, but the one that caught his eye was the extensive list of those that perished aboard Brother Jonathan. The roster was long and contained passengers as well as crew members. Seeing all of the names together impressed the magnitude of what had happened that fateful day in 1865. Erick began to slowly shake his head; there were so many, he thought. He read through the names on the list until... wait, what the—? No longer trusting his eyes, Erick moved closer and wiped the rain from the plaque with his hand. The tip of his index finger came to rest on a single entry. "I did not imagine any of this. These were real people. I saw three of their kids in the annex and chased the fourth through this cemetery. This is all REAL!" His inner voice screamed as he began forcefully tapping his finger on the entry that read, "D.C. Rowell, wife and four children." Tangled in the new revelation, Erick was suddenly jolted from the moment by a flash of lightning followed by a reverberating boom of thunder from just overhead. Looking down at his watch, he saw it was six-forty-five. He realized he had spent more time at the cemetery than he had intended. If he had any hope of getting his car today, he needed to leave now. Erick turned and began making his way back to his rental car at the other end of the cemetery. In all of the excitement, he failed to notice the additional plaque. The one just above the Brother Jonathan passenger list...the one with the entry, "St. George Lighthouse in Memoriam Keeper William Erickson October 14, 1883."

Back inside the shelter of the rental car, Erick took some time to catch his breath. On the exposed bluff, the parking lot was exposed with no protection from the full force of the winds. Erick could hear and feel the strength of the wind as it howled and buffeted the car, rocking it back and forth. Through the windshield, he stared at the whitecapped waves as they churned and heaved. The storm was literally on the front stoop knocking at the door. Erick took the steering wheel in hand, whipped the car out of the parking lot, and headed down Ninth Street towards Dick's.

Parking in front of Dick's Auto Repair, he could see the exterior lights were off, as were the interior lights, except for the flickering light from a television in the back. Looking through the spotless windows, he recalled something Jimmy had shared about Richard on that first day, "the dude has a thing about clean windows. Don't smudge the windows..." Jimmy had also joked about Richard being a window cleaner in another life. Erick never put much stock in reincarnation, but he had to confess, Richard knew about windows. Opening the front door and stepping inside, Erick hoped Richard also knew about fixing cars.

As soon as Erick got up to the counter, Richard stood up from his desk. Erick could see the large man was in the middle of a TV dinner and a tall can of Coors beer. "Was beginning to wonder if you were gonna make it. Finished your windows, not more than an hour ago," Richard said as he wiped his hands on a stained shop towel. Erick told him that he appreciated it, but it really hadn't been necessary, especially with the rain and all. With a look of conviction, Richard said, "don't mention it. It's all part of the service. No sense in saddling up if you're not going to do the job right the first time." Erick didn't want to encourage him, so he just nodded his head in agreement, hoping they could avoid the small talk and get right to the paperwork.

Richard could have been reading Erick's mind, "guess you probably want to settle up so you can get clear of this storm." Richard reached to a file under the counter and produced several papers stapled together. Richard laid the documents on the table with a pen, "like I said before, there's no charge; this was all covered under the recall of November last year. I just need your signatures where I've highlighted." As Erick went through the paperwork, Richard gestured towards the television, "you hearing this? The weatherman is saying something about a 'Bom-Bo-genesis' or something or other. Where do they come up with this stuff? Rain isn't supposed to be falling sideways." The large man stood there in the shadows shaking his head in disgust, "it's streaking the hell out of my windows, and to think they preempted Gunsmoke and The Rifleman for this crap." Erick finished signing the last of the paperwork and laid the pen on the counter. In the low lighting, the shadows transformed Richard's appearance. Erick couldn't help noticing how much the man resembled a character he recalled from an old Mel Brooks movie adaptation of a famous Mary Shelley novel. It's alive! his mind screamed. "Hey, what's so funny?" Richard said with a confused look on his face. Erick was caught off guard. He had been unaware that he had been grinning and now had to scramble for an excuse. While the image had given him a chuckle, it would have been rude and unquestionably unhealthy for him to share it with the much larger man, "...oh, it's nothing really. Just an old memory that popped into my head." Richard's eyes somehow grew beadier as he eyeballed Erick with a glare that said he wasn't convinced. Richard slowly slid Erick's car keys across the counter, "yeah, well...drive safely."

By the time Erick left Dick's, it was dark outside. Erick trotted over to the rental car. Per his prearranged agreement with the rental agent, he left the keys under the passenger side floor mat and locked the doors. With that done, he ran over and got into his Mercedes. He crumpled the shop's protective floormats and tossed them onto the backseat floorboard. After letting the car warm up, he backed up and pulled out of the parking lot. Driving south on Northcrest Drive, he glanced at the clock on the car's multimedia center screen and saw it was almost seven-forty-five. Making the right onto highway 101, he was amazed at how quickly the busy little town had rolled up the streets, turning into a veritable ghost town. As he neared the fork in the road, the rain was so intense he almost missed his turn at M Street. Slowing to a crawl, Erick saw the turn at the last minute and made the right, staying on the 101. Slowly but surely, he made his way to Ninth Street, where he made his final turn towards Aunt Mabel's.

As he approached J Street, a flash of lightning lit up the sky. Erick started counting Mississippi's to gauge the distance, but the sound of thunder never came. All of a sudden, another flash lit up the street. Erick began a new count in his head, one Mississippi, two Mississippi, three Mississippi. Erick made it all the way to his twelfth Mississippi before a third burst of light reflected off the windows of the Del Norte County Offices on his right. Pulling his Mercedes to a stop at the intersection, he glanced over at the car's GPS to get his bearings. He was at the corner of Ninth Street and H Street. Erick stared down H Street, but the rain was coming in sheets, significantly reducing visibility. Then it happened again, another explosion of bright light. The light pierced through the rain like a hot knife through warm butter. Erick realized that the flashes of light weren't bursts of lightning. Whatever the light source was, it was coming from the direction of the Del Norte County Historical Society Museum and the Bolen Annex. Erick knew the storm was getting worse. He realized the sensible thing to do would be to return to Aunt Mabel's and ride out the storm there. Still, Erick was tired of all the questions that only led to more puzzling uncertainty. Turning right onto H Street, Erick began to make his way down the four blocks to the museum and hopefully some answers.

Erick methodically closed the distance to the museum. From about a block away, he realized that the light was coming from the Bolen Annex. The same building where the First-Order Fresnel lens from the St. George Reef Lighthouse was kept. This was puzzling, though, because he was under the impression that the old lamp was no longer operational; it was merely part of the exhibit. Still, there it was in all of its glory. The old light had some impressive power for sure. Turning left onto Sixth Street, he pulled alongside the curb before shifting into park and turning off the ignition. Sitting in his car, he stared at the annex as the wind and rain howled and pelted his car like some beast trying to get at him. Erick watched as the powerful light continued on its twelve-second cyclic rotation. At this distance, Erick had to avert his gaze every time the light cycled as blinding beams of light exploded through the windows of the Bolen Annex.

Erick opened the car door and stepped into the fray. Fighting the wind, he eventually managed to get the car door closed. He pulled his jacket tightly around him and stumbled onto the curb, and crossed the sidewalk towards the annex door. It's as if the wind and rain were working together to prevent him from ever reaching the annex door. While the rain was blinding him the wind was blowing him off course. Floundering and stumbling, Erick finally reached the door. Grabbing the doorknob, he gave it a turn. The door blew open in a WOOSH! Erick tumbled across the threshold and immediately turned to close the door against the force of the wind. It took both hands pressed against the door and him leaning into the door with all his weight, but in the end, he heard the door's throw latch fall into place.

(Sunday / October 14, 1883)

As soon as the throw latch clicked into place, Erick sensed a change in the room. He didn't just perceive a difference; he also felt the shift. There were physical changes that took place that his senses registered. Before entering, there had been the blinding light of the First-Order Fresnel lens, but that had vanished. Now there was a warmer, softer glow—the type of hue a candle or lantern might cast. Erick was also aware of an unusual smell he couldn't quite place; it was a musty, oily scent. Perhaps the most confusing development thus far was the degree of familiarity he experienced because of these sensations. There was an uncanny déjà vu about it all that he couldn't explain.

As he turned towards the room, he heard the gravelly voice of curator Duffy someplace over his shoulder from behind, "here now, have a cup, laddie. Come dry yourself 'fore ya catch yer death." As Erick turned to face the room, he couldn't believe what he was seeing. This was not the annex he remembered. All the exhibits were gone, and in their place were simple rustic objects like a wooden table with three wooden chairs in place around it. At the center of the table, an old kerosene lantern casts the only light in the otherwise dark and dank room. To the right of the table stood curator Duffy still in his full uniform, holding a hot cup of chicory coffee. Erick could see the steam vapor rising from the cup. Wait a minute, Erick paused, *how did I know he would be holding chicory coffee? Why not regular coffee? Why not tea or hot cocoa, for that matter?* Erick felt the déjà vu feeling again, only this time he also began to feel lightheaded. He shuffled and lurched forward towards the nearest wooden chair. He heard Duffy place the coffee mug on the table and felt the curator grab his right arm to support him and guide him to the chair. Once Erick was seated, Duffy asked, "did ya see second assistant McCarthy lad? I sent him after ya some time back. By Poseidon! Amphitrite is shrieking! Quite the tempest out there, I hope the lads all right."

As soon as Duffy finished his comment, the door burst open with a crash, and a young man stumbled through. Erick watched the young manfight the wind for control of the door. As the youth leaned into the door, he yelled over his shoulder, "Mr. Duffy, sir! I couldn't reach the lower pier, sir; she's blowing too hard, and the seas are breaking over the pier! I've searched the entire platform with nary a sign of him, sir. I fear a rogue may have taken him over the side, sir!" As if adding a physical exclamation point to his last comment, the young man managed to slam the door before falling to the ground with his back against the bottom rail of the door. "have ya lost yer sight lad? Mr. Erickson is sitting right in front of ya. See here, Tommy!" Duffy stepped forward, slapping Erick on the shoulder, "our William has made his way back safe and sound back where he belongs." Everything happening seemed surreal. It was as if he was having another bad dream, one he couldn't wake up from. That sense of déjà vu had grown more robust. Though he tried, Erick was unable to fight whatever it was that was pushing him through the thin veil, the veil that separates a sound mind from madness. His vision began to narrow and close in as if he were traveling through a long tunnel. Erick could feel the thin veil of sanity brush across his face, over his head, and down the back of his neck, leaving only William Erickson in its wake. The last thing he remembered before losing consciousness was the sensation of Duffy's hand resting on his shoulder, "glad to have ya back aboard, William."

When he first opened his eyes, all he could see were the shadows cast upon the ceiling by the candle on a nearby table. The shadows flickered across the ceiling in a manner that made it difficult for his eyes to focus. William wasn't sure how long he had been out.

All he knew for sure was he had a splitting headache and needed a cup of coffee. Propping-up on his elbows, he stroked his bearded face with his hand and tried to shake the cobwebs from his head. Getting out of bed, he made his way across the bedroom to the small cast iron sink on the far wall. Turning the faucet, he cupped his hands under the spout and splashed cold water on his face. Next, he walked over to the window and peered into the darkness and the storm raging outside. He looked at the small calendar he kept on the wall next to the window. He had drawn black marks for each day over their standard tour of duty. They were a fortnight past their relief date with no reprieve in sight. He knew there was no hope of being relieved, so long as the storm raged on, no one would risk it. They would have to ration supplies and make do until calmer seas prevailed, but he knew that was the least of their worries. Solitude has a peculiar way about it; it does strange things to a man's mind. It pushes men to extremes. The mind latches onto thoughts it wouldn't otherwise entertain. Every man has a limit. The isolation of St. George Reef was well known for driving otherwise sane men to their limit, and a few had even ventured beyond their limit.

Standing at the window, he could hear muffled voices from the other side of the bedroom's door. He walked over to the door and placed his ear at the space between the jamb and the door. Straining to listen, he could make out that Duffy and Tommy were arguing about something. Though he couldn't understand what was being said, he could tell the conversation was growing more heated. As the two men continued their argument, William reached down and took hold of the cold metal doorknob. The rusty hinges creaked as the door gradually swung open. William stepped into the dark narrow hallway. Carefully he quietly made his way towards the light at the end of the hall, where the two men were arguing, "Mr. Duffy sir, I don't know why ya keep going on 'bout this. Ya know it weren't true of me, sir." Duffy says, "Aye, true enough...ya be mostly a good lad, but the devil he's a trickster what lies and deceives otherwise good men to sin. Take heed, boy! Ya must purge yer conscience if yer to save yer soul! Yer only hope lies in confessin' lad!" As William neared the end of the hallway, he heard the sound of a scuffle and the clatter of wood crashing and breaking. After the crash, the room went quiet except for a strange, garbled gurgling sound followed by a heavy thud.

Stepping out of the shadows of the hallway, William sees Duffy standing over young Tommy McCarthy's body. Tommy is lying face down with his head at Duffy's feet. As William stares at Tommy, he sees a bright red blood pool forming beneath Tommy's neck. William looks from Tommy's body and up to Duffy. That's when he sees Duffy is holding his old Sheffield straight razor in his right hand. William can see bright red blood running the edge of the blade from heel to tip. William gawks at the scene in shock as blood slowly drips from the tip of the straight razor to the floor beside Duffy's right boot, "it weren't my fault...I tried to speak reason to the lad...what he done... 'twas wrong!" Duffy ranted and rambled on with the wild-eyed look of a madman.

Looking down at the young man's body, Duffy staggers over and rights the overturned chair taking a seat at the table. He leans forward and trims the lamp, causing the room to darken. William watches as Tommy's lifeless body recedes into the shadows cast upon the floor by the trimmed lamp. "ya know William, they'll not understand on the mainland. They don't know what it's like fer us out here on the Dragons back. Besides, the lad done wrong. There's a price what needs payin' when a man does what he ought not. The lad had it coming, William." Cautiously, William walks over to the table. Duffy places the bloody Sheffield on the table in front of where he's sitting and looks up at William, "he ought not have done it, William! The lad had no right!" William took stock of the situation and realized being marooned on a reef in a lighthouse six miles from the mainland was a precarious position to be in. Matters were only made more tenuous because he found himself marooned with a murderous lighthouse keeper. He needed to buy some time, time enough to formulate a plan for what to do next. William figured the best way to stall was to ask Duffy to explain what Tommy had done.

William walked over to the coffee pot on the counter and poured two cups of the chicory coffee Duffy was so fond of. William asked, "can I get ya a cup?" Duffy ignored the offer, choosing instead to sit in watchful silence. Inadvertently bumping his boot against Tommy's corpse, William corrected his path and stepped around the body as he reached towards the table to place a cup in front of Duffy. As he did, Duffy's hand flew onto the table, covering the bloody razor. Moving to a chair at the other side of the table, William coaxingly said, "easy man, no need for that. Come now, why don't you close that thing 'fore ya lop a finger off." William watched as Duffy's wild eyes darted and bounced about. In the most soothing and reassuring voice he could muster, William said, "go easy, Jack... you're working yourself into a right state. Have a drink and calm yourself. What was it the lad done?" William saw the out of control fire in Duffy's eyes cool to a steadier flame; still there, yet nothing like its former self.

After drinking half the cup of chicory coffee, Duffy stared at the tabletop. He began to explain that he had confronted Tommy about stealing his wife. Duffy went on to tell William how after their last tour of duty at the lighthouse, he had returned home to find his wife had left him, taking his two sons with her when she went. Through squinted eyes, Duffy looked up from the table, "I knew it were him William, fer I kept her skin out here on the reef. Lest she get her hands on it ya see." Duffy paused and shook his head, "she's gone, William. My bonnie lass has returned to the sea from which I found her, taking my lads with her." It finally dawned on William what Duffy was talking about. The man's wife had left him, taking their sons with her. Duffy had driven himself mad with grief and had it in his mind that she had been a Selkie, or seal folk, spoken of in Scottish folktale. William was no authority on the subject, but from stories he had heard, it was believed that if a human man acquired the sealskin of a selkie-maiden, she had no option but to become his wife. The only way she could escape and return to her original seal form was if she somehow managed to recover her skin. William realized that must have been what Duffy was trying to get Tommy to admit to when he first heard the two men arguing.

The two men sat in the room with the corpse of Tommy McCarthy. Duffy tilted his head and squinted his eyes as he studied William from across the table. Though the room was dark, the lantern cast enough light that William could see something was eating at the man. There was a question begging an answer, "of course there's always the chance..." Duffy let the words linger as he tilted his head to the other side, "what if it weren't young Tommy after all?" Having sized up William, Duffy's head straightened. Duffy leaned forward, placing both hands on the table with his right hand over the Sheffield's scales, "what say ya, William. There's but one other man it coulda been." Duffy's hand closed around the Sheffield's scales with his long boney forefinger and thumb gripping the razor's shank.

As the madness in Duffy's eyes fanned into a wild and unrestrained firestorm, William knew what was next. Duffy lunged forwards across the table, swinging the razor wildly, narrowly missing William's face. Where Duffy had lunged, William had pushed, sending the table forwards into the crazed man's midsection. William heard a "hoof!" as the air was forced from the man's diaphragm. Duffy laid draped across the wooden table, gasping for air and buying William the precious time he needed to reach the door.

As the door flew open, William ran out into the storm. With no visible moonlight and the storm having knocked out all the lamps, the platform was pitch black. William knew he had no choice. He had one chance, and that was the station rowboat in the boathouse on the lower platform. Leaning into the wind, William slowly made his way by memory, towards where the stairs were that lead down to the lower platform and pier. Lightning flashed across the sky, briefly lighting the platform enough for him to adjust his course. Thunder rumbled in the distance. William turned to see Duffy's silhouette standing in the lighthouse doorway shouting into the darkness, "best cleanse yer soul William, ya no place to run lad!"

William made it to the stairs and began descending. Navigating the stairs was a risky undertaking in the calmest of conditions. In a storm like this, it was foolhardy at best, but what choice was there. With each step he took, William descended into the jaws of the furious seas. He risked being washed off the stairs by any number of large waves, let alone the legendary rogue. William stepped onto the lower platform. As Duffy descended the stairs, he called out, "oh William, how could ya let me punish poor Tommy fer yer sins, ya double cause to clear yer conscience 'fore ya face yer

Maker lad. There be a price what needs payin' William!"

William flung open the boathouse door and began dragging the rowboat across the concrete platform by the starboard gunnel. As the lightning flashed and the thunder cracked from above, he could hear Duffy singing as he made his way down the stairs,

"Oh, there were three keepers alone on a reef,

They tended the lamp alone the three,

They sent out the signal to herald the way,

A safer passage to yon Crescent Bay..."

William managed to get the boat to the edge of the ladder, which led down to the pier. He knew there was no hope of launching from the pier; the waves were simply too large and ferocious. To even attempt such a thing would only end in disaster. No, he thought, the only way I give myself a chance is to jump the next swell. William grabbed the thick mooring rope and wrapped it around his arm. It was a questionable tactic, but he couldn't risk being separated from the boat in these conditions. As the next swell rose and washed over the lower pier, William drove forward with every measure of strength he had. The boat slid over the lower platform's edge and into the black void below, taking the mooring rope and him with it.

William heard the boat splash into the rising swell only seconds before he did. It took all he had to hold off the involuntary reflex to inhale as his body reacted to being submerged in the frigid sea. When he surfaced, he floundered towards the boat before remembering the mooring rope wrapped around his arm. Grabbing hold of the rope, he reeled in the wayward skiff and hauled himself over the gunwale, and laid gasping for air. As the lightning flashed across the sky, William caught a glimpse of Duffy standing on the lower platform looking out at him as the sea carried him further away. When the lightning flashed again, William saw glints of light refract off the Sheffield's blade as Duffy pointed it at him. Duffy was screaming something, but it was impossible to hear over the roaring of the sea. Seconds later, another flash illuminated the lower platform, but there was no sign of Duffy. William surmised the sea had taken the man. William searched the boat for oars but found none. He had neglected to retrieve the oars or any life vests in his haste to launch the skiff. In a last-ditch effort, William leaned over the starboard gunwale and tried to paddle with his arm, but he realized how futile his actions were. The waves were massive, and the swells relentless. As the skiff crested one of the monstrous waves, William caught a glimpse of the St. George Reef's lamp off in the distance. But it was just a glimpse before the bow of the skiff began to tip... down...for the beginning of what would be the final plunge into the frigid black void below.

EPILOGUE

(Thursday Day 5 / October 15, 2020)

Opening the front door, Mabel and Shirley stepped out onto the front porch and surveyed the damage. The yards in their neighborhood were a mess; there was debris strewn everywhere. Fortunately for the sisters, except for a few broken tree branches littered about the front yard, they appeared to have lucked out. Holding Sir Barrymore Jr., Shirley stares across the street at the park and asked, "Mabel, I don't recall hearin' if Erick came in last night, do you?" Mabel shook her head, "no, we should call Dick's and make sure he made it there. He may have decided to hunker down there with Richard and Jimmy." Shirley agreed, and Mabel went back inside to call Richard while Shirley and Bear-Bear disappeared around the side of the house to inspect the backyard.

Mabel got Richard on the telephone and asked him if Erick ever made it there to pick up his car. Confused,

Richard asked, "Erick, who?" Mabel explained, "Erick Williamson, of course. You were working on his Mercedes." After a pause on the line, Richard said, "Mable, I don't know of any Erick Williamson. We don't even have a Mercedes in the shop. Come to think of it, I haven't worked on a Mercedes in...gosh, it must be over a year since I've had one in the shop." Baffled, Mabel asked, "you don't remember the young man you referred to us on Sunday?" "Mabel, I haven't had any business on account of this storm; therefore, I haven't had anyone to refer," he said. Mabel apologized and thanked Richard for the information. Confused and distressed, Mabel went to find Shirley.

Mabel found Shirley in the backyard and related the conversation she had with Richard. The sisters decided the only thing left for them to do was to check Erick's room. Standing outside the bedroom door, Mabel knocked and called his name. Shirley said, "Mabel, what are you doing. We know he's not in the house. That's the whole point of us searching his room." Mabel shot Shirley a glare and, in a hushed voice, chastises her, "there are procedures Shirley Dean, rules that have to be followed. He is a paying tenant, after all." Shirley just rolled her eyes and pushed the door open revealing an empty room.

Entering the room, they saw the bed was still made and unslept in. Mabel walked across the room to the closet. She opened the doors but it was empty, "have I taken leave of my senses, or did we not have a guest named Erick Williamson staying with us?" Mabel turns from the closet and sees Shirley and Sir Barrymore Jr. standing next to the bed by the nightstand, examining a piece of paper, "what's that you got there, Shirls?" Shirley flipped it over, "not sure, something Bear-Bear found between the bed and the nightstand. Looks like one of those fortunes you get outta one of them fortune machines. Doesn't Richard have one at the shop?" Mabel said, "yea, I think he might. What's it say?" Mabel crossed the room and joined Shirley by the bed. "kind of strange, 'Beware the keeper's soured rum.' It doesn't make any sense." Mabel took the card and studied it while Shirley continued to search the room. Finally, Mabel said, "Shirley, this makes more sense if you understand that 'soured rum' is an anagram. If you read it that way, it makes perfect sense; it's a warning." Mabel read it aloud, "Beware, the Keeper's Murderous." "Oh, my word, Mabel," Shirley said, standing next to the large dresser drawers at the foot of the bed over by the wall. Mabel saw Shirley was holding one of the old tintype photographs that would have been hanging on the wall ordinarily. As she joined her sister, Mabel saw the familiar picture of the two men. The older man has a long wiry beard and based on their uniforms, it was clear both men were lighthouse keepers. In the background was the unique façade of the St. George Reef Lighthouse. Mabel asked, "That the photo of the two keepers? Wonder why it's over there on the dresser and not hanging on the wall where it belongs?" Shirley removed the photograph from its frame and flipped it over. Scrawled across the back, she found the date, "September 1883." Flipping the photo back to the front, she held the photograph out for Mabel to see. Mabel stared at the picture and asked, "Shirley, we've seen this photo I don't know how many times; what's so special about it this time?" Shirley pushed the photograph towards Mabel with wide-eyed persistence, "looky there Mabel...right there between the two keepers. Tell me what ya see." Moving closer, Mabel strained to focus her eyes on what Shirley was so adamant that she see. In the background, partly obscured by a large wooden barrel. There was a third keeper, one she had never noticed before now. The man was bent over, coiling the excess of a large rigging rope hanging from something just out of frame. The third man was clearly focused on his task, with no discernable desire to have his picture taken. Still, as luck would have it, his profile was inadvertently captured for posterity along with the somber images of the other two men. In disbelief, Mabel finally recognized the third keeper, "this can't be, Shirley Dean, this is impossible." Shirley placed the photograph back in the frame before hanging it back on the wall, "guess it all depends on your definition of impossible, Mabel. 'Cause, that's definitely our Erick Williamson in that there photograph, no mistake about that. I reckon the only way this makes any sense is if you believe in..." Shirley paused, considering the keeper in the photograph, "naw, I'm not gonna be the one to say it."

◆ ◆ ◆

Afterword

The Steamer Brother Jonathan was a real ship. It's shipwreck on the Dragon Rocks of St. George Reef is well documented.

Brother Jonathan Memorial Cemetery sits at the southeast corner of 9th and Pebble Beach Dr., Crescent City, CA.

The Rowell family (Daniel, Polina or Polna, Elias, Henry, Charles, and a fourth unknown child) all perished in the shipwreck of Brother Jonathan. The author was unable to find the name of the fourth child while researching this story.

St. George Reef Lighthouse sits approximately six miles northwest of Point St. George on West Seal Rock.

Due to its' isolation and extreme conditions, St. George Reef Lighthouse was considered the most dangerous and least sought after posting in the U.S. Light Service. Unlike other lighthouses, family members were not allowed on-site. Families of those serving on the reef were housed on the mainland during tours of duty. The U.S. Coast Guard decommissioned the Lighthouse in 1975. A fully automated navigation buoy now carries out responsibilities.

The Battery Point Lighthouse sits on an island approximately 200 yards northwest of the Crescent City Harbor entrance. The Lighthouse was decommissioned in 1965 but relit in 1982 as a peresonal directional aid. Tours are available to the public during low tide.

The John Eldin character's name is an anagram for John E. Lind. John E. Lind was a real keeper who worked both the St. George Reef Lighthouse and the Battery Point Lighthouse.

The Erick Williamson character's name is an anagram for William Erickson. William Erickson was an assistant keeper at St. George Reef and vanished with the station boat while on his way to Crescent City.

The Del Norte County Historical Society maintains a treasure trove of information on their website and in their museum at 6th and H Street in Crescent City, CA. The Society also manages the Battery Point Lighthouse.

ACKNOWLEDGEMENT

Lorem ipsum dolor sit amet, consectetur adipiscing elit, sed do eiusmod tempor incididunt ut labore et dolore magna aliqua. Ut enim ad minim veniam, quis nostrud exercitation ullamco laboris.

ABOUT THE AUTHOR

Robert D. Hurley

Robert is a poet, writer, and author of the short story "The Keeper." He lives in Texas.

Made in the USA
Las Vegas, NV
10 December 2020